Cover Up
Ink It Up Book 4
Kristin MacQueen

Cover Up – Ink It Up Book Four

First edition. October 16, 2023.

Copyright ©2023 Kristin MacQueen.

Written by Kristin MacQueen.

All rights reserved. No part of this book may be reproduced in any form or by any electronic or mechanical means, including information storage and retrieval systems, without permission in writing from the author, except by reviewers, who may quote brief passages in a review.

This is a work of fiction. Names, characters, places, and incidents either are the products of the author's imagination or are used fictitiously. Any resemblance to actual persons, living or dead, businesses, companies, events or locales is entirely coincidental.

Contents

Trigger Warning		1
Playlist		2
1.	Steele	3
2.	Hannah	12
3.	Steele	20
4.	Hannah	27
5.	Hannah	34
6.	Steele	43
7.	Hannah	49
8.	Steele	57
9.	Hannah	67
10.	Steele	74
11.	Hannah	81
12.	Steele	89

13.	Hannah	95
14.	Steele	101
15.	Hannah	107
16.	Steele	114
17.	Hannah	127
18.	Steele	136
19.	Hannah	146
20.	Steele	154
21.	Hannah	163
22.	Steele	171
23.	Hannah	178
24.	Steele	183
25.	Hannah	199
26.	Steele	204
Author's Note		217
Also by Kristin MacQueen		218

Trigger Warning

Please note, this book contains some physical violence that might be disturbing to some.

Playlist

Spotify

Dark Days – Point North, Jeris Johnson
Screaming in Silence – Citizen Soldier
Afterlife – Citizen Soldier
Worth the Fight – No Resolve
Take This Pain – Jake Banfield
Still Breathing – Citizen Soldier
Hurt – GAWNE, Atlus
SAVE ME – Phix
Forever & Always – Written by Wolves
Before You Go – No Resolve, Katey x Krista
Broken Like Me – Citizen Soldier
Unwanted – Camylio
Tattoos – Citizen Soldier

Chapter 1
Steele

Leaning back in my chair, I stretch my arms over my head and try to hold in the groan begging to be released. I've been sitting on this uncomfortable stool for almost ten hours. It's too much. Too long.

"Thanks, man. This looks great. I can't wait to see what Bailey thinks." Cal glances over his shoulder at the back piece I just finished.

Calan is one of the members of Operation Riot, a popular rock band that Knox's brother is in. All four of the band members are awesome and when Knox, Damon, Rocco, and I started tattooing, they let us practice on them.

Even though they're big shot rock stars now, they still come to us for all their new pieces. They've made sure to let all their fans know where they get their ink done. Because of them we've had so many new clients. It's awesome how they've used their fame to help us really make a name for ourselves.

"How's Bailey feeling?"

"She's tired of being pregnant." Calan chuckles.

"Well, maybe you should stop knocking her up."

"Nah, I love seeing her with my baby in her belly. She's fucking gorgeous."

"Yeah, but what number will this be?"

"Five." He smirks.

"Holy shit. You're crazy."

"What? She wanted a lot of kids. I'm not going to deny my wife what she wants, especially when I love the process of making the babies." He lifts his shoulder in a shrug. "Plus, I love our little ones. I'm just hoping this one will be a boy. My son needs a friend, plus three girls are a little much, I don't need a fourth."

"Damn, you have three daughters? What are you going to do when they start dating?" Rocco leans against the wall of my cubby and watches Calan.

"Keep them away from boys like you." Calan eyes him with amusement.

"Hey now. I'm a fucking fantastic husband. Ask Pit Bull. That woman is enamored with me and my little girl is wrapped around my finger."

"Yeah, I was surprised when Quinn said how great you are for Cammie. We had to confirm we were talking about the same Rocco." Calan folds his arms over his chest and stands with his feet shoulder width apart.

"Oh, fuck off." Rocco flips him off before stomping out of my cubby.

"What did you do to the moron?" Knox frowns at Rocco's retreating back as he steps into the room.

"I'm giving him shit. He's trying to make me depressed by asking what's going to happen when my babies start dating."

"Sounds like he deserves it. No one wants to think about that." Knox rolls his eyes like it's obvious. "Quinn said there's going to be a big party before you guys leave to go on tour again. I'm looking forward to seeing everyone."

"Yeah, I was told to invite all of you. Bailey wants to talk to you, Knox. She wants a tattoo when the baby is born. She wasn't sure how long she has to wait."

"She shouldn't be breastfeeding anymore. If she got an infection, you wouldn't want the baby to get it."

"Well, damn. She might never get it if you don't keep your dick away from her. How long has it been since she wasn't pregnant or breastfeeding?" I arch a brow with a smirk.

"Since before we got married." Calan sinks his teeth into his bottom lip and shakes his head. "Don't judge me until you put your baby in a woman. I became even more obsessed with my wife and it hasn't gone away."

"One day she's going to get you neutered." Knox chuckles.

"Coming from the man who just knocked up his wife." I roll my eyes.

"This is only number one. There's no judging allowed." He folds his arms over his chest and glares at me.

"In my defense, Harley isn't Bailey's kid. So, I've only knocked up Bailey four times."

"In less than five years," I point out. "How do you even go on tour with that many kids?"

"It isn't fun, but we make it work. We're talking about getting our own bus for the next one though. It's getting a little awkward when we have to keep telling Harley that Aunt Aria fell off the bed multiple times a night because that woman is a screamer." Cal stares at us with wide eyes. "One night all three women *fell* off the bed and at least two of the guys *stubbed* their toes. My daughter's going to grow up thinking their aunts and uncles are unable to maneuver around like adults without hurting themselves."

Knox and I snort with laughter. I can only imagine how hard it is to come up with an excuse when everyone's having sex with little kids around.

"Alright, I better go so I can pick up dinner on my way home. I promised Bailey she wouldn't have to cook tonight."

"Such a wonderful husband."

"Damn straight. I make sure she's happy. Thanks, Steele. I'll see you guys later."

Calan slips me some money, then he's out the door. Whenever the guys come in, they avoid dealing with Ashley as much as they can. Not because there are bad feelings between them and her, but because they don't want to be hanging around the lobby.

It's become more and more common for people to recognize the guys from the band. Especially here. Since they're open about where they get their tattoos, I've seen people hang around outside, just hoping to catch a glimpse of them.

I can only imagine how hard it is to live that sort of life. I know it's what they're used to, but it's not what I'd want. I'm happy to lead a completely uneventful life. I don't need fame or fortune; I just want a simple life. Maybe with a woman I love by my side.

Tugging open my mailbox, I smile when I find a light blue envelope with familiar handwriting. I haven't heard from Hannah in a few weeks. It's weird to go that long without any sort of letter from her.

Over the years, she's sent me hundreds, maybe even thousands of letters. It all started while I was deployed. Hannah was part of a group of people who would spend time writing letters to people in the military who didn't have family at home to write to.

I'm not really sure how I got put on the list, but I have a feeling Rocco had something to do with it. That man doesn't know how to keep his nose out of everyone's business.

The first letter surprised me. I responded to her, but kept it brief. I figured she wouldn't write to me again and I didn't really want to grow attached to someone who was going to disappoint me like everyone else in my life had.

Hannah was different though. She wrote back time and time again. Sometimes she'd write me multiple letters before I had the chance to write her back. She's shown me over and over again how she's not going to leave.

Her letters are quirky, funny, and sweet. She's always made me feel loved and cared for, even though we've never met. Hell, I don't even know what she looks like.

We agreed early on to not share photos. I didn't want to put a face to the woman I was getting to know, or I'd definitely become attached to her. I never stopped wondering though.

Every time a female client comes in, I wonder if my Hannah is like them. Does she have blonde, brown, black, or red hair? Are her eyes as bright as her personality, or does she have deep, dark eyes? I wonder if she's tall or if I'd make her feel tiny next to my six foot two frame.

I've dreamed of meeting her and pulling her into my arms. I'm not sure I'd ever let go. Honestly, other than the guys she is one of the only other people to have stuck around.

I swear I wouldn't be able to get rid of Knox, Damon, and Rocco, even if I tried. Hell, I have tried to get rid of Rocco at least a few dozen times.

Unlocking my front door, I step inside and drop my wallet and keys in the dish on the table right inside.

Slipping my finger under the flap of the envelope, I carefully open it as I settle into my recliner.

Dear Steele,

I did it! I took a leap and changed jobs! I'm not sure if this is good or bad, but I'm going to pray it was an intelligent choice to make. I hated that stupid hospital and all of the administration. They didn't care about any of the employees and I don't want to work somewhere like that any longer.

The new place is... ok. I'm not a huge fan of my manager, but all of my coworkers are nice. The surgeons are another story. They're even more of a pain in the ass than the ones I worked with at the hospital. I'm hoping maybe it will get better once I prove myself, but I'm not holding my breath.

I wish I knew how to draw. I'd kill to work with you and tattoo people all day long. I guess it would be pretty weird for a girl with only one tattoo to tattoo people for a living, huh?

I started dating someone. He's super sweet and he encouraged me to change jobs. I'm not going to say he's the one, but I really like him.

How have you been? Anything new going on?

Hannah

I smile at her letter and take out a blank piece of paper to write her back. Sure, we could text, email, or call each other, but this is where we began and where we plan to keep things.

Hannah has my phone number. I gave it to her in case she ever needed me for something, but she's never used it. I think the idea of calling each other seems too intimate. It makes us feel too vulnerable.

But that's ok. I'm just happy to have Hannah in my life in whatever way I can get her.

Chapter 2
Hannah

Letting out a little squeal, I grab my mail out of the box and rush up the stairs to my apartment. I love getting mail from Steele. He's by far my best friend. Even if we've never met. And I don't know what he looks like. Or sounds like.

I shake my head, trying to clear my thoughts. I want to read his letter, not dream about what he looks like... but, I do. I want to know so badly. It's driving me crazy that I don't know if he looks the way I picture him.

Back to the letter!

Hannah Banana,

I'm so proud of you, sweetheart. You stood up for yourself and are finding your own happiness. That's so awesome. I hope the new place gets better. If not, let me know. I can definitely kick some ass... or get you a job at the hospital Willow works at.

Damn, if you knew how to draw, it'd be so much fun. I'd love to have you work with me. It's awesome having the guys here, but if I got to have you here too, it'd be perfection.

As far as the tattoo artist with only one tattoo, Damon didn't have a single tattoo until after Shay moved in with him. Some customers gave him shit, but they were just teasing him. Most couldn't care less, as long as you're good at your job.

This guy better be treating you like a princess, or I really will come kick some ass. You deserve someone great in your life. Someone to support you and love you.

I've been living life. It's boring now that all of the guys are married and starting families. I don't really have anyone to hang out with anymore, but that's what happens, right? People grow up and everyone begins their own lives. Now, I just need to get used to it.

At least Ashley's still single. I'm not the only one in the shop. If I was, that would be depressing. The girls always stop in to say hi or to bring the guys something for lunch. It kinda sucks to always be on the sidelines and never really having anyone in my life.

Maybe one day the perfect woman will fall into my lap, but until that happens, I'll just keep inking people.

I hope you're having a wonderful day, sweetheart.

Steele

As soon as I'm finished reading, I start all over again. I can never get enough of Steele's words. I'm always left wanting more.

I let out a long sigh. I know I should get up. Barry's going to be here for dinner soon, and I haven't even started it yet.

Since I wrote Steele my last letter, things haven't been great with Barry. He can be really moody and it's frustrating to deal with. I feel like I'm constantly walking on eggshells around him.

Last week he got pissed because I didn't have milk when he came over. He threw a glass against the wall and it shattered into a million pieces. I cleaned it up, but for days I was still finding small glass shards around my dining room.

Yesterday, he got upset that I didn't answer my phone the first time he called. He didn't care that I was at work or taking care of a very sick patient. It's so frustrating.

When I got home from work, he was leaning against my apartment building with a big smile and an even bigger flower arrangement. I feel like I'm getting emotional whiplash from him.

I thought about it all night long. I've decided I want to end things for good. He's nothing like the sweet man

I met. He's not supportive and encouraging. I thought he was, but now I feel like he's manipulating me. He supported me changing jobs because he wanted me to have less friends at work. Then I wouldn't spend time with them instead of him. He told me that when he got drunk over the weekend.

As soon as dinner is in the oven, I grab the clean laundry out of the dryer and take it into my bedroom. I'm hoping I can get all of this folded and put away before Barry gets here. Then it's one less thing I need to do if he leaves late again.

I'm just placing my last bra in the drawer when my front door opens and closes. I listen carefully to see if I can figure out if he's in a good mood or not.

"Hannah?" Barry's sweet tone brings a smile to my face. Maybe he's just been stressed with work. I know there have been talks of layoffs and he was worried he could be one of the unlucky employees.

"I'm in my room! Just finishing laundry!" I call as I gather my basket and place it in the bottom of my closet.

Walking out of my room with a smile on my face, I head towards the living room. I'm just coming into view of the couch when the timer goes off to check on the dinner.

"Hey, how was work?"

My steps falter when I find Barry reading the letter from Steele. It's not that I'm trying to hide Steele from anyone, but somehow my talking to him has always felt very personal. We don't talk about surface lawyer things as often as I would with most people. Instead, we talk about the deep things that you don't ordinarily talk about.

"Who is Steele?" Barry narrows his eyes on me, his voice is practically a growl.

"He's a friend," I say softly as a chill runs down my spine.

"How long have you been writing to him?" He folds his arms over his chest, the letter still tucked in his hands.

"I-I don't know," I stutter. "Probably close to ten years."

"Ten years?" He asks slowly, almost like he doesn't believe what he's hearing. "Why didn't you tell me you had another boyfriend?"

"What?" My brows draw together. What is he talking about? "Steele isn't my boyfriend. He's my best friend."

"Then why haven't I met him?"

"Because I've never met him!"

Barry's off the chair and standing in front of me in the blink of an eye. Before I can say anything, his hand whips across my face, stinging my skin.

I stumble back a few steps, my hand instinctively covering my cheek as I gasp and tears fill my eyes.

"Don't you dare lie to me, bitch! Do you really expect me to believe you've never met your best friend? How stupid do you think I am?"

His hand slaps across my other cheek. This time the coppery taste of blood fills my mouth. I can't hold back the tears any longer. They trickle down my cheek as I choke on a sob.

Who is this man? He's nothing like the sweet and caring man I thought I was dating. No, he's a monster.

As soon as he sees my tears, it's like a switch flips. Barry's brows pinch together and he tilts his head to the side like he's examining me.

"Hannah," he breathes my name. "Are you ok, sweetheart? I'm sorry. I didn't mean to do that. I don't know what came over me."

He wraps his large arms around me and my entire body tenses. I don't want him touching me. I don't even want him in my home, but I don't know how to get him to leave.

Hell, I don't want to date him anymore. How do I break that to him though? I don't want him to hit me again and I know he's going to flip out.

"I'm so sorry, baby." Barry covers my mouth with his and I let out a quiet whimper.

I don't want him to touch me. The thought runs through my head over and over again. My cheeks still sting and my mind is screaming at me to get out of here. Nothing good can come from staying.

A shrill alarm fills the silence and I stumble backwards until my back hits the wall. I blink in surprise, unable to keep up with what's going on around me. My head hurts so bad. It's hard to focus.

Barry's voice comes from the kitchen. A string of curse words tumbles out of his mouth as he slips on oven mitts and takes the casserole dish out. It's burnt and filling the small room with smoke.

I blink again. No matter how much I know I need to move and clear the kitchen of smoke, I can't get my legs to work. I'm stuck in this spot, watching everything happening around me. Why can't I get my body to respond?

"What is wrong with you?" Barry growls in my face.

When did he come back over here? He was just in the kitchen.

"I-I don't know," I whisper.

"Snap the fuck out of it and get the alarm to turn off." He places both hands on my shoulders and shoves me hard. My back hits the wall again, but this time the movement forces my head to slam back into the hard surface.

I collapse to the ground and hold my head in my hands. I can't focus on anything right now.

Pounding on the front door pulls my attention away from the pain. Why is someone knocking so loudly?

"You're fucking worthless," Barry growls.

As soon as his back is to me, I scramble to stand. I need to get into my room and lock the door before he can stop me. It takes a couple of tries for me to get my feet under me. I lean against the wall to help me stay standing, but I don't stop moving.

Barry's talking to someone at the door, but I can't make out what they're saying. Maybe I just can't process their words because my head hurts so badly.

Either way, as soon as I'm in my room, I quietly shut the door and flip the lock… and the other lock. I made sure I was prepared.

This isn't the first time I've had a man lay their hands on me, but this will be the last. Hopefully.

Chapter 3
Steele

Grabbing a beer out of the cooler, I lower myself into a chair and watch the chaos around us. Max, Damon's step son, is running around Rocco's yard as Duke chases him. I swear he loves that dog too much.

Achilles is watching them, but he seems comfortable where he is. He's almost like a parent, watching Rocco's puppy and making sure he doesn't get into trouble.

"He's going to sleep well tonight," Shay sighs with a content smile on her lips.

"Max or Duke?" I smirk.

"Hopefully both!" Cammie laughs. "This little bundle of baby keeps me awake enough." She rests her hands on her growing belly and grins. "If you add in how often Lanan still wakes up... I don't need Duke being up."

"Oh, please! You love that dog. Last night when I got home from work, you were cuddled up with him in our bed. I had to sleep across the foot of the bed because someone started growling at me when I tried to move him." Rocco rolls his eyes.

"Cammie or the dog?" I ask.

"Cammie," Rocco deadpans.

"Duke's probably a better cuddler than you." I tip my bottle back to hide my grin. "That's not his fault."

"No one is a better cuddler than me." Rocco glares at me. "And I don't want anyone else touching my woman."

"Be careful, Lana. Daddy's going to fight you for touching Mommy," Willow mocks him.

"She already took Cammie's tits, she can't have anything else." Rocco eyes Cammie. She has a blanket thrown over her shoulder, covering up herself and Lana while she breastfeeds.

"Oh, stop it! They'll be yours again in a few months." Cammie waves him off.

"Can we stop talking about my sister's tits?" Knox grimaces and glances away from his sister.

"You should see what happens when we're in the middle of passionate love making. Those things start leaking all over me." A devilish grin spreads over Rocco's face.

"Enough," Knox growls.

"You won't hate it when Willow starts doing it to you," Rocco singsongs.

"How'd we start talking about my boobs? I wasn't even involved in this conversation!" Willow shakes her head with amusement in her eyes. She's used to us and our crazy conversations. She knows no topic is private when Rocco's around.

"Steele, when are you getting yourself a woman?" Rocco grins at me as he lifts his beer to his lips and takes a long swig.

"Eh, I'm hoping you move away, then I can safely date without worrying about you scaring them away."

Knox and Damon snort with laughter, but Rocco's smile slips from his face. Shit. He's been a little more sensitive with my teasing lately. I think Lana's making him soft.

He rises from his seat and heads inside with an excuse to get another beer, but he just opened that one.

"What's going on with him?" Knox keeps his attention on the door, but he's talking to Cammie.

"I don't know," she sighs. "He's so focused on Steele finding a woman." She smiles sadly at me. "He keeps asking me if there are any women I can set you up with."

"I don't need his help getting a girlfriend. I haven't been looking for one." I roll my eyes.

"I know, but you know how he is. When he has something, he wants all of you to have it too." She lifts her shoulder in a shrug.

"He's exhausted," Damon says. "He's been staying up half the night working on sketches because he doesn't want to take away from his time with Cammie and Lana."

"Ah, shit. Remember how moody he used to get when we were deployed and he didn't get enough sleep?" I shake my head. "Sometimes he was worse than hormonal pre-teens."

"Too bad we can't just throw chocolate at him." Knox smirks.

"I'll go talk to him." I push myself up and head inside.

Rocco's leaning against the counter, staring into the living room like he's watching someone or something, but there's nothing there.

"You know I don't actually want you to move away, right?" I lean against the hard surface next to him and fold my arms over my chest.

"Yeah, I'm sure." He rolls his eyes.

"I'm serious, Roc. You're my best friend. You've always been there for me, even more than Damon and Knox were. You showed up to my physical therapy and pushed me to work harder. I hated you every second of it, but I wouldn't be where I am today without you. I just like fucking with you."

"Well, I wasn't going to push you around in a wheelchair for the rest of your life," he grumbles under his breath.

"I know it was you who kept me alive overseas," I say softly.

"We all kept you alive." He rolls his eyes again.

I don't know why, but Rocco refuses to take credit for saving my life. He placed a tourniquet around my leg and held pressure on my open wound after our truck exploded and my leg got blown off.

"Nah, Damon told me what really happened. It was you. I've known for a long time."

"Why didn't you say anything?"

"I don't know." I shrug, focusing on a random spot in the living room. I don't really like reliving those memories. They were hell. "I guess I figured if you didn't want to talk about it, then I wasn't going to bring it up. We both know you'll run your mouth a mile a minute when you want to talk, or you clam up when you don't."

"Then why bring it up now?"

"Because I don't think you understand how important you are to me. Not only did you save my life on the battlefield, but you pushed me to regain my independence.

Time and time again, you've gone above and beyond to save me in various ways. You always know when I need a joke to pull me out of where my mind is too."

"That's only because you look constipated when your head is in a bad place."

We're quiet for a few minutes, both of us lost in thought. I hate seeing him like this. He's normally such a happy and goofy guy. Sometimes it's hard to remember he's still human and can hurt.

"You need to sleep. You can't stay up and work on sketches after Cammie and Lana go to sleep. You're going to run yourself into the ground. We both know you'll keep going until you can't anymore and then you'll crash. You'll be no use to the girls if you're sick."

"I'm trying to make sure Cammie doesn't need to work too much."

"That's stupid, man. She loves designing. She was talking to Willow about it earlier. She wants to design more, but she feels like she doesn't have time because you or Lana are always needing attention. Take Lana and let her design, or I'll watch Lana so both of you can work at the same time. I love that little girl, you know that."

"You'd really watch her?"

"Of course. What else do I have to do?"

"If you found a woman you wouldn't have to babysit to fill your time."

"I don't need help finding a woman, Roc. Hell, I'm not sure I even want one."

"A man?" His brows shoot up and he stares at me with wide eyes. "This is a judgment free zone."

"No," I sigh. Only Rocco would assume I'm not attracted to women because I'm not dating anyone. "I don't know, sometimes it seems like a lot of work. Look at how much drama the women have brought into everyone's life."

"They're worth it. Every second of stress and drama is worth it when she stares up at you with big trusting eyes. I know she trusts me with every fiber of her being. I'm her personal knight in shining tattoos and I fucking love every second of it."

"I don't have a hero complex." I roll my eyes.

"Fine. Don't you want someone to look at you like you're their entire world? It's everything. Plus, it's nice having someone to lean on, someone who actually gives a shit about you. Everyone needs that in their life."

"Maybe, but I'd have to find someone worth the drama."

Chapter 4
Hannah

The bruise on my cheek has finally healed. I've never been so thankful for it being flu season. I've been able to wear a mask at work and no one really bats an eye. A lot of people will wear a mask to prevent themselves from getting sick, or if they don't feel good, they'll try to keep other people from getting sick.

I used it to cover up the marks my abusive boyfriend left.

I refuse to answer Barry's calls and we've been working opposite shifts for the past two weeks. I picked up shifts on his days off, just to make sure I wasn't free to do anything.

I know this can't last forever, but I wanted to give us some time apart so I could really think about what I should do. I know I need to break up with him, I just don't know the best way to do it.

Every day when I come home from work, there's something left at my door from Barry. One day it was a vase of beautiful flowers. The next was a cute little teddy bear.

Another day there was a box of cookies from my favorite bakery and another day there was a box of chocolate. Each day, the gift was accompanied with a little note from Barry. There was always an apology and a promise that it will never happen again.

I gather my mail and sort through it as I climb the stairs to my apartment. A letter from Steele has a smile making its appearance on my face for the first time in weeks. I slip my finger under the flap and open it as soon as my door is shut behind me.

Hannah Banana,

Sometimes I really wish you lived closer. I know we're not insanely far away from each other, but I wish I could stop by at the end of a long day and just chill with you. We wouldn't even need to do anything. We could silently watch TV together and eat dinner.

That sounds like the perfect night to me.

I know we promised we'd never meet each other, but sometimes I wish we could.

I hope life, work, and your boyfriend are treating you well. You know I'm only a phone call away if you ever need me.

Steele

I suck in a deep breath and blow it out slowly as I stare up at the ceiling and try to blink away the tears forming in my eyes.

I want that too. I want to spend the night curled up on the couch with Steele. It sounds amazing.

I'm only a phone call away if you ever need me.

I wonder what Steele would do if I called him and begged him to come here. If I asked him for help.

He's told me about what happened with Willow, Shay, and Cammie. He clearly cares about the women in his life and he's gone through a lot to protect them. He'd come in a heartbeat, I know it, but I don't want to pull him into this. It's not his fight. It's mine.

I take the letter into my room and place it in the second drawer of my nightstand with all of the other ones Steele has recently sent me. There's a big box in my closet with every one I've ever received, but I keep the recent ones in my nightstand. Sometimes after a long day I like to reread his letters and pretend he's here.

Once I've grabbed some clothes, I head into the bathroom to take a shower. I always feel gross when I get home from work and I like to wash the day off of me.

I make quick work of washing my hair and body before I hop out and get dressed. I don't know what I'm having for dinner tonight, but I need to figure that out. Then, I just want to lay in bed and get lost in a romance novel.

My romance life might be crumbling, but that doesn't mean I can't pretend for a little bit that I have the perfect book boyfriend.

Stepping out of the bathroom, I freeze when I find Barry lying on my bed with one of Steele's letters in his hand. What is he doing? He can't just go through my things!

"Barry? What are you doing here?" I frown at him, taking slow steps out of the bathroom.

"Well, you've been avoiding me," he says emotionlessly.

"I wasn't avoiding you," I lie. "I was working a lot. People were on vacation and I needed to pick up shifts to cover the unit."

"You could've called or texted me." He folds his arms over his broad chest and glares at me.

"Sure, but I didn't want to wake you up. I know we've been working opposite schedules."

"Why's this asshole writing to you again?" He holds up the paper and waves it in the air.

"I told you, we've been writing to each other for a decade. Why would he suddenly stop?" I pinch the bridge of my nose, more than done with him already.

"Oh, I'm sorry, am I annoying you?" He climbs off the bed and stands to his full height.

Yes. Yes, you are. I'd love it if you'd just leave.

"No. I just have a headache. I had a difficult patient today." Lies, lies, and more lies.

"Did you tell him what happened?" He gestures to the letter he dropped on my bed.

"What are you talking about?"

Barry snatches the paper off the bed and snarls at it.

"Did you tell... Steele about how I tripped and slapped you by accident?"

Tripped? Is he seriously trying to act like that was an accident? It was anything but an accident. He meant everything that happened that night. I have no doubt if someone hadn't knocked on the door and I hadn't locked myself in my room, things would've gotten worse.

"No. I haven't had a chance to write back to him," I say slowly. Barry's face hardens and I quickly add, "Plus, our relationship is none of his business. I don't ask questions about his girlfriend."

Mostly because she doesn't exist.

"Then why is he saying he hopes I'm treating you right?" He takes a step towards me and I flinch.

"Because he cares about me. He constantly sends letters saying he hopes work and life are treating me well. I'm like a little sister to him."

He takes another step and I have to fight to keep myself from reacting. Every cell in my body is screaming at me to run and get away from him, but I'm positive he'd chased me, and it would only make things worse for myself.

"I don't like him. I want you to stop writing to him."

"No." My brows furrow. Who the hell does he think he is?

"Excuse me? I said I want you to stop writing to him. Stop talking to him entirely."

I've been talking to Steele for almost half of my life. There's no way I'm going to cut him out of it now. Not for an abusive man I've known for less than six months.

And I'd never abandon Steele. Not after his past. No, I refuse to be another person who's going to disappoint him. I won't be part of that long list. I want to be on the short list of people he can count on. The one that up until a year or two ago, only had five other names on it. Now that Shay and Willow are in the picture, Steele's list is getting a little longer.

"I'm not going to stop talking to him, Barry. He's my best friend. He's been there for me through some of the hardest parts of my life."

"I'm not losing my woman to some asshole who likes to play the hero," he growls.

"Get out of my apartment. I'm done. I don't want you to come back and I don't want to hear from you again."

As soon as the words are out of my mouth and a deadly glare settles across Barry's face, I know I've made a mistake.

I expect him to slap me again or maybe push me. I don't see the hard fist aimed straight for my jaw. My head snaps to the side with the momentum and I cry out in pain. Before I can lift a hand to hold my face, he hits me with another punch. This time I stumble and fall onto the floor. On my way down, I hit my head on the corner of my nightstand and everything goes blurry.

I welcome the blackness slowly taking over. If it swallows me into its darkness, I won't feel any of the pain raining down on my body.

Because if there's one thing I know about Barry, he's not going to stop unless someone makes him. He's going to keep hitting me.

Chapter 5
Hannah

Blinking my eyes open, I squint at the harsh bright lights. I try to cover my face with my hands, but my arms don't seem to want to cooperate with me. It takes me a few minutes before I'm finally able to get my eyes to open.

The chilly room is void of any sort of color or personality. The walls are white, as is everything else. I swallow hard when I hear the rhythmic beeping of a machine and memories of what happened flood my thoughts.

"Hey, how are you feeling?" A woman in scrubs enters the room slowly. Her voice is soft and caring, she's trying not to scare me.

"Sore," I whisper hoarsely.

"I'm sure you are. I can get you some medication, but I'd like to ask you some questions first. Is that ok?"

I try to nod my head, but the movement makes pain shoot through my skull. I wince as I rest my palm softly on my head. This is going to be a rough recovery.

"Yes."

"You know what, how about I get the medication now? After you take it, we can talk for as long as we can before you fall asleep. The questions can wait, I care more about your pain level."

"Is my phone here?" I glance around the room. There's only one person I want to talk to.

"Yes, the paramedics found your phone in your pocket and they gave it to us. I'll get it."

She disappears and comes back a few minutes later. After she administers the medicine into my IV, she asks me a few questions and promises me there will be more questions later on.

The police have already been here to question me, but I wasn't awake. They asked the nurses to call them when I woke up, but she's going to give me a few more hours before she does.

"How did I get here? I hit my head. I can't imagine Barry stopped hitting me. He only ever stops if something pulls his attention away from me." I frown down at my hands.

"Your neighbor heard you scream a few times and Barry yelling. He called the police and banged on your door. He said this wasn't the first time?"

"No. He hit me two weeks ago. That was the first time."

"Do you want to talk about it? I'm no stranger to domestic abuse." She smiles sadly.

"Did you get away from it?"

"I did, but it was one of the hardest things I've ever done. My ex was a big-time lawyer. When he lost a case or had a bad day, it got taken out on me. I knew if I reported him and nothing came of it, he'd kill me. There's no way he'd want anyone to know his true colors." She shakes her head and takes a moment to compose herself.

"What'd you do?"

"Well, I knew one of his cases was particularly hard and he wasn't sure he was going to win the lawsuit. And that never boded well for me in the past. We had those little cameras on the outside of our house, so I brought them into our living room and placed them in all four corners. I made sure I was sitting in the living room when he got home so the cameras would be on me. I didn't provoke him or anything, I just let the night progress naturally. I knew what he'd do and this way I had it on camera. There was no way he could smooth talk his way out of evidence."

She lifts her shoulder in a small shrug, but I can see the memories still impact her. "He almost beat me to death that night," she whispers.

"I'm so sorry," I say softly.

"I'm not. His overly violent behavior was caught on tape and I was able to get him thrown into prison because of it. The judge and jury took very little convincing because there was no way for him to argue what was on the screen. Cameras don't take feelings or thoughts into consideration, it records your actions. That's all people needed to see to know he was guilty. He was charged with attempted murder and sentenced to prison."

"What happens when he gets out?"

The sad smile she's had on her face since she began talking slowly slips. She shakes her head and tears brim in her eyes.

"He won't be getting out. He put a lot of people in prison. One of them was serving a life sentence and found out he was there. He convinced some inmate that was kept in the same area as my ex to beat him up enough to get him sent to the infirmary. The man cut himself so he'd be sent as well and when the nurse left to get some bandages, he stabbed my ex over and over again. He didn't stop until he was dead."

"That's horrible! I'm so sorry!"

"It is, but he's not the man I married. He's not the one who promised to love and cherish me forever. That man died a long time ago. Part of me is upset over what happened to him and how he died, but the other part of me is relieved I won't have to worry about my safety when he gets released from prison. I ruined his career and his future when I recorded his attack on me, when I hired a lawyer, and took it to court."

"I started dating Barry a few months ago. He seemed great in the beginning. He was supportive of me leaving my job and finding a new one at a smaller hospital. I thought that was so sweet, until I realized he did it so I didn't have as many friends to hang out with. He wanted me with him all the time. Two weeks ago, he hit me after he found a letter from a friend. I've been talking to Steele for about a decade. He was in the military and didn't have family so I started writing to him. We've never met, never even talked on the phone or texted. Our only communication is through letters, but he's become my best friend. Tonight, Barry found another letter from Steele and he demanded I stop talking to him. I told him no and to get out of my apartment. I don't want to date him anymore... he flipped out and punched me twice. I hit my head and my memory starts getting fuzzy after that."

"When the police come, you need to tell them all of this. Especially if you want to keep him away. You could get a restraining order. You could possibly press charges, but I'm not sure. Clearly law is not my field."

"Would I be able to make a phone call before these meds kick in?"

"Of course. Just press this button if you need me." She points to the small red button on the side of the bed, then leaves quickly.

I suck in a deep breath and blow it out slowly. I can't believe I'm doing this, but I really want to talk to him. And not through letters.

I scroll through my phone and find his contact information, then hit call before I can chicken out. The line rings once, then twice before it clicks.

"Hello? Hannah?" His deep voice rumbles and wraps around me like a warm blanket. How can a voice I've never heard before feel like home?

"Hey, Steele," I say softly.

"Are you ok?"

"Yeah, I'm ok now. I just... I don't know. I wanted to talk to you without waiting days for a response. Is that ok?"

"Sweetheart, that's more than ok. I told you to call me anytime you needed me."

"I really needed to hear your voice."

"I can talk for as long as you want." His deep chuckle fills the line. "I just got home from work and started making dinner. What are you up to?"

"I'm at the hospital."

There's a long pause on the other end of the line before Steele's voice comes through again.

"As an employee or patient?"

"Can we talk about anything else? I don't want to talk about it right now."

"I can come to you. If you need me, I'll be there as fast as I can."

"No, I don't want you to worry about me."

"Hannah Banana, you're one of the most important people in my life."

The way he says my nickname has butterflies filling my stomach and making it hard to focus on anything else.

"I made your short list?" I smile at the thought and how many times I've teased him about his short list.

"You're at the top of my list, darling."

"You're the only name on my list," I confess with a bit of hesitation. I'm not used to being vulnerable with people.

It's easy to be raw and real with Steele through letters. I don't have to utter a single word and I can almost detach myself from the situation because he's not there, this is so much harder.

"Hey, don't be trying to one up me." The smile in his voice has a grin spreading across my face. "Are you going to tell me what's going on? You've had my number for over five years and you've never called."

"I'm sorry, maybe I shouldn't have called. I can let you go if I'm bothering you." Gone is the teasing and lighthearted conversation and in its place is an uncomfortable tension that's making my chest ache.

"Don't you dare hang up on me, Hannah. I don't want to admit how happy I am to talk to you on the phone because I'd sound pathetic, but we both know something is going on or you wouldn't have called. Can I please come see you?"

"No," I whisper as tears fill my eyes. I don't know what I look like right now, but I guarantee it isn't pretty. His first impression of me shouldn't be when I'm battered and broken.

"You're killing me. I'm worried about you."

A man walks into the room with a white coat on. The left side of his chest says Dr. Stevens. He smiles and waits patiently for me to finish my phone call.

"Steele, the doctor just came in. Can I call you back tomorrow?"

"Shit, darling. What hospital are you at? I'm coming."

"Please don't. I'll call you tomorrow."

"Fine, but if you don't, I'm coming to find you."

"Please do. Bye, Steele."

"Goodbye, Hannah."

I blink away the tears that are threatening to spill over. I didn't expect to feel so emotional after talking to him. I can only imagine how I'll feel if we ever actually meet.

Chapter 6
Steele

I run a hand through my hair and grip the back of my neck. What the hell is going on? There's no way she called me because curiosity got the best of her and she wanted to know what my voice sounded like. Something is wrong.

I pace the length of the living room and try to decide what to do. I could go to her apartment, but that isn't going to help if she's in the hospital. I snatch my phone off of the coffee table where I dropped it after Hannah hung up. Quickly opening my internet, I search for what hospitals are closest to her apartment. There are five within thirty minutes of her.

"Fuck, she could be at any of these."

My mind races with every possibility. She could've been in a car accident. She could've had someone break into her apartment. Maybe she got mugged.

"I can't do this," I murmur as I pull up my contact list and press call. I'm not sure if I should be calling him, but I need someone to talk to.

"Hey, what's up? Are you ok?"

"No, I don't know what to do. I'm struggling."

"Do you need me to come over?" Rocco asks quickly. Keys jingle in the background and I have no doubt he's already slipping on his shoes and telling Cammie he'll be back.

"No. No, I'm fine. I just needed someone to talk to."

"And you chose me?" The surprise in his voice is clear as day and I feel a little bad about that.

Rocco might be crazy and slightly annoying... ok, really annoying... but you can always count on him. He'll drop everything in a second and rush over to you. He loves and cares with his entire heart. You get all of him or none of him.

"Yeah, I told you, you're my best friend."

"Shit, I thought you were just saying that to make me feel better."

"Should I call Knox instead?" I sigh.

"No! Don't you dare call that fucker! I'm here. Tell me what's going on."

"Hannah," I breathe her name like a prayer as emotion washes over me. "She called me."

"I didn't think you had each other's phone numbers. Have you ever spoken before?"

"Nope. We exchanged numbers in case we ever needed each other, but we've kept our communications to strictly letters."

"Did she tell you what's going on? What's your gut say?"

"She said she was at the hospital, but she won't tell me if she's working or a patient. My gut is saying something is fucking wrong."

"Do you want me to go with you? We can just check on her."

"I don't know. She said the doctor just came in and she'd call me back tomorrow. There are five hospitals within thirty minutes of her apartment. She could be at any of them... What do you think?"

"I think if she's saying she'll call you back tomorrow then you should wait to talk to her. I know this is hard as fuck, but if she's in the hospital, then she's safe and being taken care of. You don't want to go all cave man on her the first time she calls you."

"Is this what you'd do if this were Cammie?" I ask, knowing he'd already be halfway to the first hospital demanding to see her.

"Hell no! If my Pit Bull was in the hospital, I'd be lying in the hospital bed beside her, but you're not me."

"What's that supposed to mean?" I frown, not sure I like what he could be implying.

"I'm needy, I don't know boundaries, and I've followed Cammie around like a lost puppy since we met. She never would've called me if she were in the hospital, we both know that. In fact, she would've told Knox not to tell me she was there at all."

I snort out a laugh because he's completely right. Cammie never would've wanted him to come visit her, not before they got together. She wanted nothing to do with him back then.

"You're not me, Steele. You'd give her a chance to come to you again. But I guarantee if she doesn't call you tomorrow, you'll be ripping this state apart looking for her. Hell, you probably told her that already."

"I said if she didn't call me, I was coming to find her," I grumble under my breath.

"See! I know you too well." I can hear the grin in his voice. "If she doesn't call by the time you're finished work tomorrow, then call her. If she doesn't answer, we'll all go find her. Deal?"

"Yeah, but I don't like this."

"You don't have to like it, you just have to do it."

"So, I just have to sit here and worry about her all night and all day tomorrow?"

"Yeah, kinda. Though, you could come over and babysit Lana so I can fuck my wife."

"Goodnight, Rocco," I growl.

"Night." His chuckle fills the air as I hit end and drop down on the edge of the couch.

I scrub my hands over my face and blow out a long breath. I can't do this. There's no way I can sit here all night and worry about her.

Steele: Can you just let me know if you're safe?

As soon as I hit send, nervous energy fills my body. What if she doesn't answer? What if she gets annoyed at me for reaching out? What if-

Hannah Banana: I'm safe, Steele. I'll call you tomorrow night, I'm in bed already. Thank you for worrying about me.

Steele: Always.

I blow out a long breath and my mind drifts to Hannah lying in bed. Now that I've heard her sexy voice, I can't stop thinking about what she must look like.

We agreed on not seeing each other in person or sending pictures to the other, we wanted this to stay totally anonymous… well, as anonymous as possible. We still know each other's names, addresses, and phone numbers. We know intimate details about our lives, but we don't know anything superficial.

Now, I'm dying to catch a glimpse of what she looks like. A peek at the woman who's occupied my mind more than any other.

I want to meet Hannah Foley.

Chapter 7
Hannah

The doctor wanted to keep me overnight for observations. He said they didn't believe there were any issues they missed, but he wanted to be sure.

Barry did a number on me. He gave me three badly bruised ribs, a black eye, a swollen jaw and face, and a whole array of colorful bruises over the rest of my body. No matter how I try to move, I'm in pain.

The cops believe Barry kept beating me until the neighbor knocked on the door. He might have continued until he heard the police sirens. All we know is he was long gone before the cops arrived and he didn't go out the door.

I'm lucky the neighbor heard my screams and cared enough to do anything. Otherwise, I could be dead right now.

I begged the doctor to let me walk home. I didn't really have anyone to call to pick me up. I could've called Steele and I know he would've dropped everything to come, but

I don't want him to see me like this. A battered and bruised face isn't the first impression I want to make.

I turn the corner and stop a few buildings down from mine. Standing on the front steps of my building is Barry. His focus is on his cell phone, he hasn't seen me yet.

"No. No, no, no. This can't be happening."

I lift my cell phone and quickly call the officer who gave me his number yesterday. My hands are shaking so badly I'm having a hard time pressing the correct numbers.

"Officer Richards," he answers on the second ring.

"Hi, this is Hannah Foley."

"Hey, Hannah. How are you feeling?"

"Not great. I just got released from the hospital and Barry is standing outside of my apartment. Could you or another officer meet me here? I don't know what he might do."

"I'll be there right as soon as I can. Keep as much distance as you can from him. I'm about five minutes away. If I get there before he leaves, I'll arrest him. He hasn't been home since he assaulted you. We have an officer sitting outside of his house and there's been no sign of him. We're going to get him."

"Thank you."

I hang up and slip my phone into my pocket. I don't know what to do. I have nowhere to hide, nowhere to wait until the officer comes. I could hide down the alley, but that doesn't sound safe either. There's a coffee shop across the street, but he'd see me if I tried to go in there. I plaster myself against the corner of the building, half hiding myself from his view.

"What am I going to do?" I whisper under my breath. "I can't go to work like this. I'm going to be a sitting duck in my apartment."

I search my contact list, trying to think of who I could stay with. I'm terrified of him coming back to my apartment and breaking in. I never gave Barry a key, I don't even know how he got in yesterday.

"Hannah!" His voice breaks through my focus and my entire body goes still. "Hannah!"

His feet pound against the pavement as he closes the distance between us. I lift my gaze and watch him. Twenty yards separate us. Ten. Five. Three. One.

"Why haven't you been answering my calls and texts?"

He reaches out a hand to touch me and I flinch, taking a step back.

"Don't touch me," I hiss.

"C'mon, Hannah. We need to talk. I've been waiting for you to come home so we could talk this out."

"You're kidding, right?"

"It was an accident. I didn't mean to hurt you." Barry rolls his eyes like I'm being ridiculous.

"You put me in this hospital, Barry!"

"I didn't mean to, baby. It was an accident. Remember? Maybe you aren't remembering what happened correctly."

"Go away, Barry. I don't want to talk to you."

"No! I need you. I can't lose you!"

Something at the intersection draws Barry's attention. His eyes widen, then he turns a pissed off glare on me.

"You called the fucking cops? Seriously? I'm not letting you go, Hannah. I'll be back for you when no one is watching."

He takes off and sprints down the alley before I can do anything else. I'm not chasing him, that would give him exactly what he wants and I want to avoid being alone with him for as long as possible.

"Hannah?" Officer Richards approaches me slowly.

"Hey." I try to smile, but my body is tired. The adrenaline rush of seeing Barry took a lot out of my already exhausted body.

"Where is he?"

"He saw your car at the intersection. He darted down the alley."

"Dammit. I've never met someone so difficult to catch." He shakes his head. "I don't think you should stay here alone. Is there anyone who could stay with you? Or that you could stay with? It would be better if you had somewhere to go for a few days, especially if Barry doesn't know them."

One name pops into my head. He's the only one I would feel safe with. I know he'd do whatever it takes to keep me safe too.

"There's someone I might be able to stay with... could you come up to my apartment with me and stay for a few minutes while I pack a bag? I promise not to take long."

"Hannah, you can take as long as you'd like. I'm not going to leave you alone in there," he says softly.

Officer Richards follows me up the stairs and waits for me to unlock the door. After I was taken away in an ambulance, he grabbed my keys and brought them to the hospital. He wasn't sure if anyone else had keys and he didn't want me locked out. He's been so kind to me.

"Thank you for doing this," I say as I glance around my apartment. I don't feel comfortable in my own home anymore.

I quickly move from one room to the next and grab what I need. I throw everything into three duffle bags and bring them out to the living room. I packed the essentials and anything of value, including my letters from Steele. I don't want anything important left behind in case Barry breaks in again.

"I'm all done."

Standing outside of the building, I glance up at the sign and blow out a long breath. I can't believe I'm here. I can't believe I'm actually going to do this.

A man walks out of the shop and holds the door open for me with a sympathetic smile. I'm sure he's noticing my bruises and he's coming up with all sorts of conclusions.

I enter the shop because I don't know what else to do. I'm already here and I have nowhere else to go. I just need to take this leap and hope everything turns out well.

"Hi! Can I help you?" A woman behind the desk smiles at me.

"Oh, uh... I'm here to see Steele."

"Awesome. I think he's still with a client, but let me check."

She disappears down a long hallway and reappears a few moments later.

"He's almost done with his client. You can follow me and wait in his cubby. He'll be with you shortly."

Once she's shown me where his cubby is at the end of the hallway, she leaves me alone. I glance around the space and take in all of the small details. The three-quarter walls are covered in sketches. They're all so different, but every one of them is amazing. Most of them are tribal designs, but some aren't.

Steele told me he loves tribal tattoos. He enjoys inking those designs more than others. He has real talent. It makes me want a tattoo. Maybe I could have him cover up my current tattoo.

Noise draws my attention to the entrance to the cubby. A soft gasp leaves my lips when my gaze lands on the man watching me. His tall frame and broad shoulders are taking up the entire doorway, making me feel so small in comparison.

His hair is short on the sides and longer on the top. It's slicked back, making him look so handsome. He has a thick beard, that's kept neat and trimmed. His exposed arms are covered in ink, but it's his pale blue eyes that have captured my attention.

Holy shit. Is this Steele?

Chapter 8
Steele

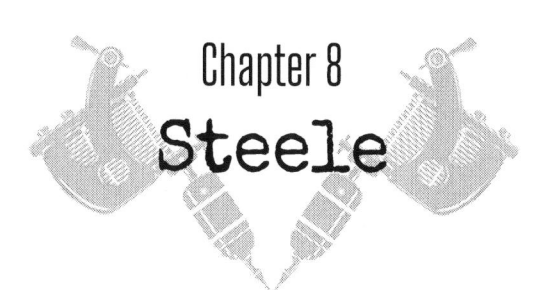

"Hey, Steele?" Ashley knocks on the door.

"You can come in. I'm finishing up," I call through the closed door. My client wanted an under the breast piece, but she's fully dressed now.

"There's a woman here looking for you. I don't have anyone else on your schedule for the day though. Do you want me to find out what she wants?" Ashley peeks her head into the private room.

"Can you just have her wait in my cubby? I'll be out of here in a few minutes."

"No problem." She smiles before shutting the door behind her.

"You outdid yourself. This is gorgeous." Tamara looks at herself in the mirror. She's wearing a low enough cut shirt that it shows off her new tattoo.

"Thanks. Are you going to call me when you want that thigh piece?"

"Of course! I just need to pick up a few shifts of overtime." She chuckles. "I swear I should just sign over my paychecks to you."

"I wouldn't turn them away." I grin. "You can take your time getting ready to go. I want to find out who this mystery person is."

"Sounds good! Thanks again! I'll leave your tip with Ashley."

"Thanks, Tamara."

I exit the private room and walk towards the last cubby. Sometimes people show up hoping they can get a tattoo squeezed into my schedule. There are times I allow it and times I tell them to fuck off. It all depends on my mood, if I have anything going on, and their attitude.

I stand in the doorway and freeze. The woman sitting on my table is covered in bruises. Her head snaps my way when I mutter a string of curse words under my breath. I clench my teeth at her black eye and swollen jaw. Who the fuck did this to her?

I don't want to upset her and I definitely don't want to make her embarrassed by her injuries though. So, I drop onto my stool and roll a little closer to her like I would any other client.

"Hey."

"Hi," she whispers softly.

My brows furrow as I try to figure out where I know her voice from. I've heard it before, but I don't know where.

"Ashley said you were asking for me."

"I'm sorry, I probably shouldn't have shown up unannounced." She wrings her hands in her lap.

"It's fine, it happens sometimes. What type of tattoo were you looking to get?"

She shakes her head, then winces. "I'm not here for a tattoo. I needed to see you… in person."

"Hannah," I breathe her name and her eyes fill with tears.

I'm off my chair and gently pulling her into my arms in the next second. I can't believe she's here. More than anything, I can't believe how beat up she is. What the hell happened?

The thought of anyone hurting this sweet woman has me wanting to bash someone's skull in. How could you lay a hand on any woman?

"I'm sorry for just showing up."

"Don't be. Are you ok?"

Her body shakes in my arms with her sobs, and her tears quickly soak through my shirt, but I don't care. Nothing else matters except the woman in my arms.

"Yes... No. I'm horrible."

"It's ok, darling. You're here now. I'll take care of you." I hold her as tightly as I can without hurting her and squeeze my eyes shut.

It feels so good to have her in my arms. She feels like she's meant to be here. Like she's my missing piece.

"Hey, Steele. Did you hear from Hannah yet?" Rocco walks into my cubby without knocking or seeing if I'm with a client, as usual.

"Yeah, I guess I have." I glance down at her, then back up at Rocco. His eyes widen and he quickly scans her body, seeing the same thing I saw. Someone beat the shit out of her.

Hannah pulls away and swipes at her cheeks with the back of her hands. She lets out a quiet hiss. I'm sure she's in a lot of pain.

"Hannah, this is Rocco," I keep my voice soft. I don't know what happened to her, but I don't want to scare her.

"Hey, sweetheart. I hope you're staying for a while. I'd love to get to know you." The normal teasing Rocco is nowhere to be seen. In his place is the gentle man you want for this type of situation. He'll make sure she feels safe and cared for. He won't do anything that could make her uncomfortable or nervous.

"I don't know yet. I don't know what I'm doing."

"Roc, I'm done for the day. I'm going to take Hannah home with me. I'll call you later about that job we were talking about."

"Ok. Hannah, it was nice meeting you."

Rocco disappears and I turn my full attention back to the girl who's lived in my heart for a long time.

"Are you comfortable coming to my house? If not, we could go somewhere more public."

"No, I'd rather not be in public. I know you'd never hurt me."

"Good." I hold my hand out to her and grin when she takes it without hesitation. She really does trust me. "C'mon, darling. Do you want to follow me or come in my car?"

"Can I come in your car? I just need to grab my bags."

"Are you staying with me, Hannah Banana?" I tease her.

"I-I don't have to. I just... I don't want to be anywhere near my car or my apartment. I'm scared he's going to find me." She glances away from me and I can tell she's embarrassed.

"You can stay with me for as long as you want to. I'll protect you."

"Can I get you anything to drink?" I ask as soon as we're in the living room.

Hannah was quiet the entire drive here and I didn't push her to talk. I kept her hand in mine, silently letting her know I'm there for her.

"Could I have some water?"

"Of course."

I grab two bottles of water out of the fridge and enter the living room. I don't know where to sit. She's sitting in the middle of the couch and I'm not sure if she'll be comfortable with me sitting next to her or if she wants space.

"Are you ok with me sitting next to you?" I motion to the empty space.

"I'm not scared of you, Steele. You'd never hurt me." There's no question in her voice, she firmly believes she can trust me and she should. I wasn't lying when I said she's one of the most important people in the world to me.

"I'm glad. I can't even stomach the thought of hurting you."

I take the seat next to her and hand Hannah her water. Giving her a few seconds, I wait while she takes a sip before I begin questioning her.

"What happened, sweetheart?"

"Remember that new boyfriend I thought was so sweet?" She smiles sadly at me.

"Are you fucking kidding me?" I growl. I'm surprised when she doesn't cower away or flinch. "Why would he do this to you?"

"Because of you," she whispers softly.

"What?" I rear back like someone just slapped me across the face. How is this my fault?

"Barry came over two weeks ago for dinner. He saw one of the letters you wrote me on the counter..."

She goes on to explain what happened and my stomach rolls with nausea. When she starts to tell me about last night, I have to fight to stay in my seat. I want to find this asshole and give him a taste of his own medicine.

"Hannah, I'm so sorry this happened." I shake my head, not understanding how anyone could do this

"What? Why are you shaking your head?"

"You chose me. You knew he'd lose his shit and you still chose me. I don't even understand that."

Hannah slips her small hand into my large one. She intertwines our fingers and scoots closer.

"You're the one thing I refuse to lose in my life. I'm not going to be someone who tosses you aside. I'm here to stay forever," she whispers, rubbing her thumb over the back of my hand.

"You can't go home until he's caught."

"I know. I'm not sure I want to go home even if he is caught. I don't feel safe in my apartment. He got in there by himself and I'm not sure how."

"What about your job?" I ask softly.

"I hate it." Her eyes fill with tears and as much as I want to give her space, I can't.

"Come here, sweetheart." I tug her against my chest and hold her.

I let her cry in my arms until I can't take the uncomfortable pain in my leg any longer. I can only wear my prosthetic leg for so long before it's painful.

"I'm sorry, but I can't stay out here any longer. I'm in too much pain."

"What's wrong?" She pulls away and stares up at me with wide eyes.

"My prosthesis. At the end of a long day, it always hurts."

"I totally forgot. Do you want to take it off?"

"Yeah, but then it's hard to move around." I grip the back of my neck. I don't like talking about my leg or the challenges I face.

"Hey, what do you normally do when this happens?" Hannah places a hand on my thigh and looks into my eyes. She has the most beautiful green eyes with small flecks of gold.

"I lay in bed and relax until it's time for me to go to sleep."

"Then let's go." Hannah rises to her full height. She holds her hand out to me and helps me stand.

"You're going to lay in bed with me?" I arch a brow and stare down at her. She's tall, but she still barely comes to my nose. It's the perfect height difference.

"Unless you don't want me to. I could find a hotel. I'm sure there's one not too far away."

"Hannah Banana," I chuckle and shake my head. "Stop it, sweetheart. I'm trying to make sure you're comfortable. You just went through something traumatic and I want to make sure I don't make it worse."

I cup her cheek and let my thumb softly graze over her bruised skin.

"I'll tell you if you're doing something I don't like. Will that help you relax?" She places her hand on my chest, right over my heart, and I promise myself right then and there, I'll do whatever I have to do to keep this woman in my life forever.

Chapter 9
Hannah

I slip under the covers of Steele's bed and press my back against his headboard. It's padded and so comfortable. I swear it's nicer than my couch at home.

Home. That place doesn't feel like home anymore. I don't feel like I have a home.

You have Steele.

The thought rushes through my mind and I quickly push it aside. That's crazy. I barely know Steele.

That's not true and you know it.

I shake my head, trying to focus on what's going on around me and nothing else. Steele slowly unbuttons his dark jeans and lowers the zipper. He peeks up at me through his lashes and I realize it's probably rude of me to be staring at him.

"Oh, sorry! I guess I shouldn't be watching you get undressed, huh?" I wrinkle my nose and watch a sexy, lopsided grin spread across his lips.

"I couldn't care less. After being in the military, I've learned to not really care who's around." He lifts his shoulder in a shrug. "But I want-"

"I am. I'm completely at ease around you," I cut him off before he can get his full sentence out.

"You might not want to see my leg." He grips the back of his neck again and my heart aches for him.

Steele is one of the sweetest people I've ever met. He's spent this entire night making sure I felt safe. And now, he's worried about bothering me.

"I'm not scared, Steele. I'm a nurse, remember?"

"Right." He blows out a long breath and lowers his jeans. They easily slide down his legs and pool on the floor.

I take in his tight boxers and his muscular body. His prosthetic starts at his upper thigh and sympathy washes over me. He lost so much by fighting for his country. I hate how so much of his life has been affected.

"I know it's not pretty, but when I take this thing off," he motions to the fake leg, "it's even uglier."

"Stop it, Steele. You're amazing. I don't view your amputation as a deformity or a handicap. I see how you fought to stay alive. How you were persistent. You had to learn to walk all over again. You went through so much since you came home. I see strength and determination when I look at you, not a broken man."

He keeps his eyes on me, but he doesn't say anything as he slides the prosthesis off and places it next to the bed. He slowly lowers the liner that protects his skin from the hard plastic. He's waiting to see my reaction to his marred skin, but he won't see one. This doesn't bother me.

Steele hops into the bathroom and washes the liner. When he comes back out, he watches me as he hops back to the bed. He sits on the side and slides himself back until his shoulder is pressing against mine.

"You're still not bothered?" He motions to his leg. There's a nasty scar stretching across his skin. It's red and irritated, I'm sure from wearing the liner and prosthesis all day.

"It's no uglier than my face is right now." I motion to myself and flash him a sad smile.

"You aren't ugly, Hannah Banana. You're gorgeous. So much prettier than I could've imagined."

"You're only saying that to make me feel better. My face is swollen and all different colors, especially with this black eye."

"How are your ribs?" He ignores my comment, but the look he gives me tells me he thinks I'm being ridiculous.

"They're sore. The doctor said it's going to take a while to heal. There isn't much I can do to help it." I shrug.

"Can I take a look?"

I scoot down in bed, until my head is on the pillow and I'm lying flat. Lifting the hem of my shirt, I tug it up until it's resting right below my bra.

"Fuck, that has to be painful," he says softly. He reaches out and brushes his fingers over the bruised skin.

Instead of pain, I feel tingles. Everywhere he touches me makes me feel like I'm alive. There's something so special about Steele. He's so different from any man I've ever met. I've always been drawn to him in a way I haven't been to other people.

I feel like our connection is stronger because we knew each other on such an intimate level before we met. It's like I know everything about him, and I'm just now putting a face to the man.

"I'm so sorry this happened to you, darling. I hate that it's my fault. I wish I had been there to stop him."

Steele leans down and softly kisses my skin. He continues tracing his fingers softly along my bruises as I run my fingers through his thick hair and watch him.

It feels like things are moving so quickly between us. Like we're too comfortable around each other, yet it feels right. Natural. Like I've known Steele forever.

"I don't. I wouldn't want you to get hurt," I whisper.

"Hannah Banana, do you really think I couldn't take Barry on?" He peeks up at me with a grin. I love how he keeps using that silly nickname. It reminds me of all the letters I've gotten over the years.

I like how he's not trying to act like our past doesn't exist. I know plenty of people who will talk to you through texts or emails and act like your best friend, yet when you're in person, they act like they don't know you at all.

"You don't know Barry. How would you know if you could overpower him?" I'm teasing him, but he doesn't know that.

Steele has four inches and at least thirty pounds of muscle on Barry. I have no doubt he could have protected me and he would've if he'd been there.

"C'mon, Banana. I could've overpowered him without breaking a sweat."

"Easily. You have a lot more muscle." I play with his short hair, massaging his scalp as I go.

"I swear, if you keep doing that, I'm going to fall asleep."

"Go ahead, I don't mind."

"I'd squish you when I fell asleep." He chuckles. "You wouldn't be able to handle anything pressing against your abdomen... How are you sleeping? Are you having nightmares?"

And there's the man I know. The one who asks the difficult questions that most people shy away from. The one who cares about more than surface level things. The man who stole my heart soon after we started talking to each other.

"I'm not sure. Last night they were giving me a lot of pain meds. I think that helped me sleep the most. I don't remember having any nightmares though."

"There's a guest bed you're more than welcome to stay in down the hall."

I glance at the door and nibble on my bottom lip. I really don't want to be alone. I'm still scared Barry's going to come after me. I know Steele would protect me, but what if he doesn't wake up or hear me?

"Or, you can stay with me. Hell, you can sleep next to me and cuddle the whole night for all I care. I'll do whatever makes you feel safer." Steele scoots up in bed so his head is hovering over mine.

"What do you want?"

"I want what's best for you... but I'd probably be happier with you in my arms so I know you're safe." He cups my cheek and leans down to press a soft kiss to my forehead. He's so gentle and caring, a complete opposite of what I'm used to.

"I'd be happier in your arms too," I whisper.

Chapter 10
Steele

I blink my eyes open and gaze down at the beautiful woman in my arms. I can't wait for her bruises to go away and for her ribs to heal. It's not that I find her unattractive or anything like that, I just want to know she isn't in pain. The bruises are a constant reminder this is my fault. I hate it.

"Are you just going to stare at me all morning?" Hannah murmurs against my chest.

Her hand is lying across my stomach and she's cuddled up as close as she can get. I don't think I've ever slept as well as I did last night and I know I have her to thank for that.

"I don't know. It's hard to tear my gaze away from a beautiful woman, especially when she's in my arms."

Most people would say our relationship is moving dangerously fast, but how is it fast when we've known each other for an entire decade. I know her deepest darkest secrets. I know her hopes and dreams. Her favorite food and how she hates cereal because it gets soggy. I'm certain I know this woman better than any other person.

Over the years, I've wondered if we met, would we end up dating. It's hard to have this raw and intimate relationship with a person and stay just friends. Maybe that was why we both agreed to stay away. Neither one of us was ready for that step yet.

Now, I'm rethinking my position. I think I'm ready.

"Are you always this sweet?" She peeks up at me with sleepy eyes.

"Fuck no." A deep chuckle shakes my chest, making her head bounce.

"Ow, your muscles hurt." She rises off of my chest and frowns down at me.

"I'm sorry my muscles hurt you." I grin. "The next time you see Rocco, ask him if I'm always sweet. He'll give you an honest answer."

"Then why are you so sweet to me?"

"You're my Hannah Banana. I don't know how to be anything else to you."

"Do you have to work today?"

"I do, but you could come with me."

"Really? Are you sure?"

"Definitely. You can watch me work, or you could go check out any of the guys' or Sammie's work too. No one cares about having an audience except if they're in one of the private rooms. You wouldn't be able to go in there."

"What happens in the private rooms?" She wiggles her brows, looking incredibly adorable.

"People get their dicks, clits, or nipples pierced. We do tattoos that are placed in private locations, like your hip, breasts, ass, or low on your pelvis."

"Do you pierce those places a lot?" She stares at me with wide eyes.

"More often than you'd imagine." I chuckle.

"Do you have any piercings?"

"Sadly." I nod my head, remembering just how I got those piercings.

"What do you mean sadly?" She tilts her head to the side and examines me.

"Well, Rocco and Damon started tattooing before Knox and I did. I was busy recovering and Knox was taking care of Achilles and helping me out. The other guys would help whenever they were free, but they were ready to be busy and they had nothing holding them back. One night, Rocco came over and I was taking a lot of pain meds at the time. I wasn't fully aware of what was going on around me and Rocco wanted to practice piercing... I ended up with pierced nipples and I didn't even know it until I woke up the next morning."

"Are they still pierced?"

"Yeah." I sigh and run my hand through my hair. "I figured I already endured the pain, I might as well keep them."

"Did he pierce anything else?" She glances down at my blanket covered crotch and I smirk.

"Nah. I've made a point to keep my dick covered when Rocco's around. He pierced his though."

"Steele! I didn't need to know that!" She swats at my chest.

"But you needed to know if mine was?" I laugh, pulling her back down to me and wrapping my arms around her. "What am I going to do with you, Hannah Banana?"

"Cuddle with me every night?" She peeks up at me.

"Always." I press a soft kiss to her forehead, letting my lips linger longer than necessary. "What else?"

"Let me see your nipples." She grins.

"If you really want to..." I trail off as I release her and sit up just far enough to pull my shirt over my head and toss it to the ground. I fold my hands behind my head and relax.

Her gaze roams over my newly exposed skin and she nibbles on her bottom lip. I want to tug her lip free and claim her mouth, but I'm afraid of hurting her. I don't want to do anything until her injuries heal. Then she's mine.

She runs her fingers over a scar on my left side. It's almost four inches long and the skin is raised. I got cut during a mission and Knox had to stitch me up. It hurt like hell, but I survived.

Her fingers trail up my chest and over my nipple. She's mesmerized by my body; her eyes never leave me.

"I always thought about getting my nipples pierced, but I never did it."

"Why?"

"I don't know. I guess I didn't feel comfortable showing my tits to some random person, especially a random guy. I don't know many female tattoo artists."

"If you want it done, you could do it whenever you want. Sammie would be happy to fit you in if you want a female to do it. And if you just want someone you know, I can do it."

"That's not weird?"

"What?"

"Seeing my boobs?"

"Eh, I've seen my fair share. I wouldn't be looking at you from a sexual perspective. It would be work. I'd be doing my job."

"I don't think I could do that." She frowns.

"Don't you see people naked all the time as a nurse?"

"Yeah, but that's different." She waves me off.

"How?" I chuckle. "We're seeing them naked for a reason and just to make it clear, I'm never seeing someone completely naked. I keep as much of their body covered as I possibly can."

"I don't know. It just feels different."

"Ok." I roll my eyes, but I'm smiling. "Let's get up and we can stop somewhere to grab breakfast before we head to Ink It Up. If you want to meet Sammie and the guys, I can text them and tell them we'll bring breakfast for everyone."

"Um... aren't you embarrassed about the bruises?" She motions to her face. "Your clients will see me."

"Sweetheart, I'm proud of you for surviving and for leaving a bad situation. No part of me is embarrassed and you shouldn't be either. You didn't choose to be beaten up by some asshole. He's the one that should be embarrassed by his actions."

"What if someone thinks you did this to me?" She's nibbling on her bottom lip again.

"Then that's their issue, not mine. If they're going to assume the worst of me, they can feel free to go fuck themselves. Clients can find someone else to tattoo them too."

"Can you just explain the situation when they get there, then I'll come in? I don't want them to be staring at me and wondering what happened."

"If that's really what you want, then yes. But they don't need to know your business."

"I'm positive. If they're your family, then I want to meet them. And I want to spend the day with you, but I'm not hiding what happened. I won't let Barry have any control over my life."

Chapter 11
Hannah

I watch Steele get out of bed and take in his glorious body. I don't know how he looks like this after years of being out of the military. I've known so many people who once they're released from their duty, they let their bodies go and enjoy freedom. But not Steele. I think he might be in better shape than the people I know on active duty.

"Do you want me to get your liner for you?" I climb out of bed, more than happy to help him. I move so I'm standing right in front of him. He's doing so much for me, I want to return the favor.

"Sweetheart, I've been living alone since I was discharged, I'm fully capable of doing everything myself."

"I didn't mean it like that," I whisper, dropping my gaze to his chest as my cheeks blaze with embarrassment. "I just want to do something to help you after everything you're doing for me."

"I'm not doing anything for you." He lifts my chin until our gazes meet and I suck in a sharp breath. His pale blue eyes capture my attention and make it impossible to look away.

"You're letting me stay here. You're holding me all night long so I feel safer. I'm basically being your shadow."

"You don't need to earn your stay, Hannah Banana. You've always had a spot in my life and that's not changing, now you're just physically here. You're in my home instead of just being in my heart."

"Dang, you weren't lying about breakfast." Rocco's face lights up when we walk into the shop with several bags in hand.

"Obviously I wasn't lying. Why would I lie about breakfast?" Steele frowns at his friend. It's funny to see him with other people. He seems so much more growly than when it's just the two of us.

"Ignore the grouch, Hannah. He has a resting dickhead face ninety-nine percent of the time. How are you feeling?" Rocco holds his arms open and smiles when I step into them and hug him back.

"Get your hands off of her." Steele elbows him in the ribs and steps around him to put the bags on the counter.

"Damn, I was just hugging the girl. You don't need to start hurting people." Rocco glares at Steele, but as soon as his back is turned, he winks and flashes me a big grin. I have a feeling he starts a lot of shit and loves every second of it.

"You don't need to hug her. She's gotten plenty of hugs since she arrived," Steele growls.

"Is someone jealous?" A man with short dark hair and thick stubble covering his jaw steps into the small lobby and glances around. His eyes land on me and hold for a few seconds.

He's wearing a tight t-shirt and dark jeans with combat boots. He looks every bit the part of an ex-SEAL. He looks downright scary with the way he's looking at me.

"I'm not jealous, but he doesn't need to touch her. They barely even know each other." Steele glares at him.

"Fuck, I was just giving her a hug hello. You don't own Hannah Banana." Rocco rolls his eyes.

"Don't call her that," Steele hisses.

"Why? You do!"

"And I'm the only one allowed to." Steele folds his arms over his chest, preparing for a fight.

It's almost comical to see the change from the man I woke up next to this morning and the man standing in front of me now. He's so protective of me. I didn't expect that.

"Ah, this is all making more sense now." The guy nods his head before turning his attention back to me. "I'm Knox. It's nice to finally meet you. I've heard so much about you."

"You have?" My brows raise up my forehead.

"Well, it's not a lot of information, but Steele's talked more about you than any other person on the planet, so it feels like that little bit is a lot." He grins. "I'd give you a hug, but I'm kinda afraid he might punch me and my wife would get a little upset if I came home with a black eye."

"What the fuck, Knox!" Steele shoves him away from me and places his hands on my arms. "Ignore the idiot. You're beautiful even with your black eye," he says softly. He cups my face and his thumb brushes over the discolored skin below my eye.

"Holy shit," someone whispers, but I can't place the voice. I'm too focused on the icy blue eyes staring into mine to care about anyone else.

"How did we miss this?" Someone else asks quietly.

"Because you're all idiots," Knox says. His voice is more distinct than the others.

"I'm not upset. He didn't offend me." I place my hand on Steele's chest, trying to get him to calm down. His heart is racing beneath my palm and I love feeling the strong steady beat.

"Good morning!" A woman singsongs and steps into the room.

"Hey, Sammie. I brought breakfast." Steele holds my gaze for one more second before stepping away and continues to unpack the food.

"Morning, Steele." She stands on her tiptoes and presses a quick kiss to his cheek. The second her eyes fall on mine, her mouth falls open, but she quickly recovers and a genuine smile spreads across her face. "Hey, I'm Sammie."

"I'm Hannah, Steele's friend."

"It's so nice to meet you." Sammie wraps me in a gentle hug. "I'm here if you need someone to talk to," she whispers in my ear before letting me go.

"Thank you, but I'm ok. Steele's been a great support and help."

"He's a great guy." She grins.

"Hey! Why can Sammie hug her without getting abused?" Rocco folds his large arms over his chest and glares at Steele.

"Because she doesn't have a dick," Steele growls.

I've noticed the man growls a lot when we're not alone. I kind of like it. He's this alpha in public, but a total teddy bear with me.

"Hey now. Have you confirmed that? Because Sammie's more of a dude than most guys I know." Rocco points at her and she rolls her eyes.

"Well, I'm certain my wife doesn't have a dick." Another man steps into the lobby. "I've pierced enough dicks to know she doesn't have one. And enough clits and tits to know she's got those. Plus, I knocked her up a couple of times so..." He trails off like he's bored with this conversation.

"Cole, this is Hannah." Sammie introduces us. "She's friends with Steele and is going to hang out here today."

"Hey, it's nice to meet you." Cole gives me a quick hug before disappearing down the hallway.

"What the fuck! Cole hugged her and you didn't lose your shit." Rocco motions wildly to me.

"Cole doesn't notice anyone other than Sammie. He'd be asexual if she didn't exist." Steele waves him off.

"He would not!" Sammie laughs. "He dated plenty of women before me."

"Hey, I'm Damon. I'm assuming you're Hannah?" Another man approaches me with an easy smile.

"Yeah, how'd you know?"

"Eh, there are few people Steele's going to be protective of and you're at the top of the list." He gives me a quick hug and then steps up next to Steele to talk to him.

"Seriously, Steele! Damon hugged her too! And he definitely has a dick. I've seen it hundreds if not thousands of times! It's not as nice as mine, but it does exist!" Rocco tosses his arms up in the air and lets them fall to his sides.

"He's been in love with Shay since before he knew what to do with his dick, therefore he doesn't count." Steele winks at me.

"This is totally unfair." Rocco's brows form a deep crevice between them.

"Fine, let me change my statement. Rocco Reeves isn't allowed to touch Hannah. Is that better?"

"Holy fuck! I have a wife and a kid! I'm not going to try anything."

"Oh, please! You'd still offer to tattoo or pierce her, just to piss off Steele." Knox chuckles.

"I only did that to Cammie because I was in love with her. Fuck, when are you going to get over the fact I'm married to your sister?"

"Never." Knox grins.

Chapter 12
Steele

"Are you ok? Is this too much for you?" I ask as soon as we're alone in my cubby. I have a few minutes before my first client is scheduled to arrive.

"I'm perfect. Your friends are amazing and were so welcoming." She steps closer and wraps her arms around my waist, resting her head against my chest. "Thank you for everything, Steele. I'll never be able to thank you enough for making me feel so at home in your life."

"Well, if you stay here long enough, I might not let you go," I whisper into her hair. It smells like something fruity, and I wonder if it's her shampoo or some sort of body spray.

She giggles and pulls back far enough to stare up at me. "How did some lucky woman not snatch you up yet?"

"It's the resting dickhead face. Rocco tells me all the time that I'm scaring away people because I don't know how to smile."

"You smiled a lot last night and this morning."

"That was because I was with you, sweetheart." I place a soft kiss on her forehead and hold her a little tighter.

I can't wait until her ribs heal. Then I won't have to be as careful about hugging her or holding her while we sleep.

"Mr. Camron, are you saying you like me?" She grins up at me.

Before I can answer her, Ashley's peeking her head into my cubby. "Hey, your client's here. I'm going to send him back, ok?"

"Yeah, sure." I sigh. I want more time with Hannah. I want to answer her question, but now I don't have time.

"What's up, fucker?" Owen Powell saunters into my cubby and plops down on my table. He swings his legs back and forth. When his gaze lands on Hannah, he freezes and his legs slow to a stop.

"I'm going to run to the bathroom. I'll be right back." Hannah ducks out of the room and I blow out a long breath.

"Who the fuck did that to her? Please tell me you killed the asshole." Owen stares at the doorway with a frown.

"Her boyfriend. We've been talking to each other for years, but never met. She showed up yesterday after she was released from the hospital and he was waiting at her door."

"You have a thing for her?" He watches me carefully as I set up my supplies.

"I'm not sure. We just met."

"Nah, you just said you've been talking for years. It doesn't matter when you met in person. I think you're head over heels for the girl and that's why she's here with you and not sitting at your house." Owen smirks.

"Does it really matter how I feel? She's getting out of an abusive relationship. The last thing she needs is to enter into a new relationship."

"No, the last thing she needs is another guy to treat her like shit. But I know you won't do that. You'll put her on a pedestal and make sure she feels like a princess. You'll treat her the way a woman should be treated."

Owen's quiet for a few minutes, which is very unlike him. When I glance over my shoulder, I realize Hannah's behind me and he probably shut up when she reappeared.

"Come sit next to me, Hannah Banana." I pat the stool I stole from one of the private rooms. I know there aren't any tattoos scheduled in them today so it's just going to be sitting in there.

Hannah settles on the stool and rolls a little closer. She's watching every move I make and I love the attention.

Normally I don't want it, but with her, I want all of her focus on me and no one else.

"Wow, did you make this design?" Hannah looks at me with shock as I remove the stencil from Owen's leg.

"Yeah, I make all of mine."

"Who did your tattoos then?"

"I've had at least one done by everyone in the shop. Knox specializes in realism, Damon in watercolor, and Rocco in portraits."

"What about Sammie and Cole? Did they do any?"

"Oh yeah. They're amazing. They can do basically anything."

"Damn straight. Sammie's one of the best I've ever seen. That girl can do anything. Right, Sammie!" Owen yells loud enough that he knows she can hear him.

"We both know I'm not going to blindly agree with you, Powell!" She yells back.

"I was saying how amazing you are!"

"Oh. Well then sure, I agree with that."

He grins and settles back so he's leaning on his hands. "See, she's awesome."

"I think someone has a crush." Hannah smirks.

"Oh shit." I roll my eyes, knowing what's going to come next.

"Hell no. Don't get me wrong, Cole's a lucky man, but no woman can top my Sunshine." Owen shakes his head and begins scrolling through his phone. When he finds a photo, he thrusts the phone in Hannah's face with a proud smile.

"She's beautiful. You two look so cute together."

"Owen's creepily obsessed with his wife." I roll my eyes.

"Fuck off. There's nothing creepy about the way I love Carrie."

"Wow, I'm surprised you know her name. I don't think I've ever heard you refer to her as anything other than Sunshine." I smirk.

"Maybe I should go to Sammie for this tattoo. She'd do a better job anyway." Owen narrows his eyes on me, but we both know he isn't serious.

"Do you have any other tattoos Steele's done?" Hannah draws Owen's attention away from me.

"Yeah, he did the tribal on my chest and one arm. Do you want to see?"

"Definitely."

Owen whips off his shirt. I swear the man doesn't care who's around. He'll strip without being asked twice.

"It's gorgeous," Hannah whispers.

"Hey, now. Don't be flirting with me. Sunshine wouldn't like that." Owen grins.

"She was talking about the ink, asshole," I growl.

"You have your nipples pierced too."

"Too? Do you have yours pierced? Or does Steele?"

"Don't ask her about her fucking nipples!" I put the needle to Owen's skin and enjoy the hiss of pain he releases.

"Motherfucker. I'm going to stop talking to her if you're going to make it hurt this much."

"Good. She doesn't need your attention."

Chapter 13
Hannah

It's been so much fun spending time at Ink It Up today. The guys are all great and so is Sammie. I've been going from one artist to the next and watching them work. Each of them are amazing and I don't know who I'd want to tattoo me more.

"Do you have any ink?" Sammie asks as she cleans up from her previous client and prepares for the next one.

"I have one... but it's embarrassing."

"Oo, now I want to know what it is." She grins.

"It's a name on my upper thigh, right below my butt cheek." I wrinkle my nose. "I hate it, but what am I supposed to do, it's a tattoo."

"You could get it covered up." Sammie shrugs. "Any one of us could cover it... but I wouldn't ask Rocco to do it."

"Why? Do you think he'd touch or do something inappropriate?" My brows furrow. I can't think of another reason I wouldn't want Rocco.

"No! Nothing like that. Rocco was a huge flirt before, but the guys were too stupid to realize he mostly only flirted with Cammie, or to piss off people. He's only ever had eyes for Cammie."

"Then why wouldn't I want Rocco?"

"Because Steele would kill him." Sammie laughs. "He wouldn't be able to handle Rocco touching you, especially your ass."

"I don't know why he's so protective," I say softly.

"Well, I can say from experience, he's being overprotective because he likes you. Cole kinda went crazy protective when he realized he was in love with me." Sammie shrugs.

"You think Steele's in love with me?"

"I think he's unaware he's in love with you."

I open and close my mouth several times, unable to find a response. I don't know what to say.

"Listen, I've known Steele for a while. Not as long as you, but long enough. He doesn't let many people get close. We're coworkers and friends. I know I can count on him for anything, but there are still walls between us because he doesn't want to let me in all the way. I understand that, so I don't push him. But you? I've heard Steele mention you a lot over the years. There's always this level of awe and wonder. It's like he can't comprehend what he did to deserve you in his life, but he's not going to ask questions. I think he's in love with you and is terrified you're going to walk away. Which I understand more than anything."

"What am I supposed to do?"

"Well, I guess that depends on how you feel. If you like him as more than a friend, then I think you should make that known. I don't think he'll make a move unless he knows how you feel."

"He's the most important person in my life," I whisper.

"But do you like him as more than a friend?" Sammie watches me carefully. She's the type of person I wish I had by my side. The best friend I've always wanted and could never find. Maybe if I stay here, we could become better friends.

"Yes," I murmur quietly enough so no one else will hear me.

"Then show him how important he is to you."

"How was your day?" Steele glances over at me as he pulls out of the parking lot of Ink It Up.

"It was so awesome. Thank you so much for letting me hang out with you." I grin at him.

"You can come hang out with me every day." He holds out his hand and as soon as I place mine in it, he brings my hand to his mouth and presses a soft kiss. Then our joined hands rest on his thigh.

"You're going to get bored of me sooner or later." I roll my eyes.

"I don't think I'll ever get bored of spending time with you, sweetheart." He flicks on his turn signal and takes a right before he continues, "Do you want me to get takeout or make something for dinner?"

"Can you cook, Mr. Camron?" I wiggle my brows, making him laugh.

"I can hold my own in a kitchen."

"Well, I want to see this." I swallow hard, knowing what I'm about to say is crossing a line and I won't be able to take it back. "There's nothing sexier than a man who can cook."

Steele's attention snaps to me for a few seconds before he stares straight ahead and focuses on driving.

"Huh? Is that so?" He asks slowly.

"Yup! You know how everyone has a fantasy they want to come true?"

Steele's brows shoot up his forehead and his eyes widen. I can only imagine the thoughts running through his head. "Yeah? What's yours?"

"Waking up in the morning to my man making me breakfast. He's barefoot and shirtless. Only wearing either boxers or jeans. He'd lift me onto the counter, steps between my legs, and kiss me until I'm breathless."

"Oh," he says softly and I instantly wonder if Sammie was all wrong about Steele's feelings.

"But I guess you don't want to hear about that. Just ignore me." I wave him off and turn my attention out the passenger's window.

Steele's silent the entire way home and when he turns off the car, he spins to face me and doesn't release my hand.

"I'm never going to ignore anything you share with me. I want to hear every thought and feeling you have, but you surprised me, Hannah Banana. Our conversations have always been via letters. I had time to formulate my responses and really think about how I was going to write back."

"I didn't go too far?" I scrunch up my nose.

"Never. You could tell me a whole erotic fantasy you have and I'd happily listen, though it might make us both uncomfortable when I get turned on." He chuckles.

"Well, I told you my fantasy, now you have to tell me yours." I grin.

"Fuck, this is opening a whole can of worms I didn't expect." He laughs and shakes his head. "Give me a few minutes to think about this while we get inside."

"Fine." I roll my eyes, but I can't hide my smile. I love how he just goes with the flow. But even more than that, I love how he really thinks about his answers and doesn't just say whatever comes to mind first.

Chapter 14
Steele

Fuck. How am I supposed to cook for Hannah now that I know she finds it sexy? The entire time, I'm going to wonder if she's staring at me and thinking about us as more than friends.

Don't get me wrong, I'd love nothing more than to have Hannah as more, but I don't want to do anything that could jeopardize our friendship. I can't lose her, she means too much to me.

I toss my keys and wallet into the dish on the table inside the door, just like I always do, then head straight to the kitchen. I'm starving and want to get dinner started right away.

"What can I do to help?" Hannah asks as I pull out meat and veggies.

"Nothing. Sit your pretty ass on the stool and watch."

"There seems to be a theme today. All I ever do is sit on a stool and watch." She sticks out her bottom lip in a pout and it's taking everything in me to stay on this side of the island and not close the distance between us. I want to kiss her and suck her lip into my mouth. I want to hear her moan and beg for more.

"Well, you're a guest." I clear my throat. "Guests aren't supposed to help."

"I don't want to be a guest." She rolls her eyes.

"Are you moving in permanently, Hannah Banana?" I quirk a brow.

"Obviously I can't just invite myself to live in someone else's house." She chuckles.

"So, are you saying if I invited you, you'd move in?"

"You're not going to want some random woman living with you. Plus, I can't sleep in your bed forever and when I peeked into your spare bedroom, there's no bed. It's only gym equipment."

"First off, you're not a random woman, you're my Hannah Banana. Second, you can sleep wherever you want. If you wanted the spare room, I could sell the gym equipment and get a gym membership instead." I shrug like changing my routine and home isn't a big deal. If it means I get to keep her here forever, I'd gladly do it though.

"Eventually you're going to have a girlfriend and she's not going to want us sharing a bed, but I don't want you to change around your home for me." She blows out a long breath. "I don't know what I want to do yet, I just know I don't want to go home unless it's to pack up my shit."

"I don't think a girlfriend is going to be an issue anytime soon. I don't really go out now that the guys are all taken and I'm not actively trying to find someone. So, unless a woman magically falls into my lap, I don't see it happening."

"You better make sure there aren't any tripping hazards around you at work or you might have a few women falling into your lap." She grins.

"Oh, please. My resting dickhead face keeps most of them away." I take out a cutting board and begin slicing the meat and veggies into thin strips.

"And what about the ones who don't take the hint?"

"I growl and bare my teeth at them." I give her my best impression of a rabid beast and she bursts out laughing.

"I think you're just a big teddy bear." She smirks at me.

"Only with you, sweetheart." I wink at her and turn my attention back to my knife before I cut myself.

"Aww, I feel special."

"You should. You're at the top of my special people list."

"Oh my gosh! This is delicious!" Hannah lets out a small moan as she takes another bite of food.

"I'm glad you're enjoying it." A slow smile spreads over my face. I love having her here and having someone to eat dinner with and spend time with.

"You know, you never answered my question earlier." She points her fork in my direction.

"What question?"

"What's your fantasy?"

"Damn, I thought you were going to forget about that." I groan, scrubbing a hand down my face.

"Nope! Spill it!"

"Fine." I grip the back of my neck and prepare myself for this awkward conversation. "Can I write it in a letter and mail it to you?"

"Not a chance!" She giggles and shakes her head, her chocolaty hair swishing all around her shoulders.

"My fantasy would be a woman who, before bed, straddles my lap and talks to me about our day. She'd be wearing a thin tank top with panties and nothing else. Her hair would be falling in my face and I'd act annoyed with it, but secretly I love it. She'd kiss me and tell me how much she loves me, then when it was time to go to sleep, she'd cuddle up against my side. Her head would rest on my chest with her arm across my stomach and her leg thrown over my thigh. She'd be as close to me as she could possibly get and every morning, she'd wake me up with a gentle kiss that would leave me begging for more."

"That's your fantasy?" Hannah's eyebrows raise high.

"See, this is why I didn't want to do this. It's embarrassing." I grab my fork and shove another bite of food into my mouth.

"You shouldn't be embarrassed. That might be the sweetest thing I've ever heard. Most guys would say something like fucking a porn star against a wall of windows." Hannah rolls her eyes. "Or tying up a woman and getting to do whatever they want to them. I love that your fantasy is more emotional and less sexual. So was mine." She lifts her shoulder in a small shrug.

I watch her carefully for any sort of humor in her words or a hint of her teasing me, but I don't find any. She seems like she actually likes what I said and I'm not sure how to feel about that.

"How do your ribs feel?" I ask after a few minutes.

"They're doing better." She nibbles on her bottom lip, trying to keep herself from smiling.

"What? Why are you looking at me like that?"

"You always ask me how my ribs are when you want to change the conversation. It's adorable, but I wonder what you're going to do when I'm all healed?"

My heart beats a little fast in my chest with the thought of her staying long after she's healed. Could she really be looking to stay? Would she seriously move in with me?

"I guess you're going to have to wait and find out."

Chapter 15
Hannah

I can't believe I'm doing this. I'm crazy, there's no other explanation. I might as well have a big neon sign on my forehead that says 'I like you'. But that's not exactly true. Even though I don't want to admit it, even to myself, I more than like Steele Camron. I'm fairly certain I fell for him years ago, but I never thought anything could come of it. I mean I never planned on talking to him on the phone, let alone meeting him in person.

And now I am about to cross every line in the sand.

Steele's lying in bed with one hand tucked behind his head, holding his kindle in the other and reading a book. I briefly wonder if he's ever read a romance novel, but I'm not going to ask him.

I slowly move around the bed, trying not to draw attention to myself. I don't want him to catch onto what I'm doing until it's time.

I climb onto the bed and move closer. Taking a deep breath, I pluck his Kindle from his fingers and steal it before he can stop me. I gently place it on my pillow before straddling his hips. I catch his brows drawing together in a frown, making him look adorable. I look down to see his lips part, but no words come out. Settling into place on his lap, his hands instinctively grip my waist and stay there.

"What are you doing, Hannah?" His gravelly voice makes my heart beat a little faster. I still can't believe I'm doing this.

"I wanted to talk to you," I whisper.

"What do you want to talk about?" He swallows hard, his eyes never leaving mine.

"I want to know how much a tattoo costs."

"It depends on what you're getting done and how long it takes to do. Why?" He frowns at me again.

"I think I want one, but I'm trying to decide if I have enough money to do it." I nibble on my bottom lip.

Steele's hand cups my cheek and he uses his thumb to pull my lip from between my teeth.

"You don't need any money for a tattoo. Just tell me what you want and where you want it. I'll do it for free, or if you'd rather someone else do it, they'll do it for free too."

"No, I need to pay." I shake my head, and place my hands on his chest.

"No. It costs barely anything for supplies, it's all the time. I don't charge the guys if I do a tattoo for them or their girls, so they wouldn't charge you. But depending on where you want it, you can't go to Rocco." He frowns again.

"Why do you hate Rocco so much?"

"I don't. I love him like a brother, but he knows how to push my buttons and he loves to do it."

"So, him touching me would push your buttons?"

"More than you know," Steele growls.

"I'd want something right here..." I grab his right hand and move it until he's gripping right below my left ass cheek.

"Motherfucker." He squeezes his eyes shut and takes a deep breath. "Yeah, Rocco can't tattoo you there. In fact, none of the guys can. You can pick me or Sammie, no one else."

"Why?" I'm pushing him, trying to get him to admit he has any sort of feelings for me so I don't feel like this is all one sided.

"Because you'd have to take your pants off and I'm not sure I can handle any man touching what's mine," his voice comes out so deep and raw, it's making my heart hammer against my sore ribs.

"Am I yours?"

"Not yet," he says softly.

"Why not?"

"Because I'm terrified of losing you."

Before Steele can say anything else, I lean down and cover his lips with my own. I'm not afraid of making the first move now that he's admitted to wanting me.

He freezes for half a second before he's kissing me back. His right hand grips my ass a little tighter and his left snakes around my waist, tugging me closer to him. I slip one hand into his hair and toy with the silky strands as Steele traces his tongue along the seam of my lips. Opening my mouth, I groan when his tongue makes contact with mine. He tastes sweet and minty, it's driving me crazy.

We kiss until we're both breathless, then I pull away and rest my forehead against his.

"Holy shit, Hannah," Steele whispers.

"Am I yours now?"

"Fuck yes, I'm not letting you go."

After kissing Steele for a little bit longer, I climb off of him and begin getting ready for bed. I want to get into his arms as soon as I can.

I pile my hair on the top of my head and begin washing off my makeup. I'm able to hide some of my bruising, but most of it is still at least slightly visible.

"You know, I have something at the shop that might be able to cover your bruises." Steele steps up behind me and wraps his arms around my waist. He rests his chin on my shoulder and meets my gaze in the mirror.

"You do?"

"Yeah. There's this concealer type stuff that can cover up tattoos and make it look like you don't have any. If it can cover black ink, I'm sure it can cover bruises." He shrugs. "I know you don't like seeing the bruises."

"I hate them," I whisper softly. "It's a constant reminder of him."

"Well, you don't have to go back there unless you want to. You're welcome to stay here."

"Yeah? For how long?" It's meant to tease him, but the way his face grows serious has me swallowing hard.

"Forever?"

"You're going to get tired of me." I grin and shake my head. How else am I supposed to respond?

"Never." He presses a soft kiss to my neck, then reaches around me to grab his toothbrush and toothpaste.

I follow his lead and we make faces at each other in the mirror while we brush our teeth. As soon as we're both finished our nighttime routine, we climb into bed.

"Get your sexy ass over here." Steele motions for me to come closer. "I'm really liking this thin tank top and panties outfit," he murmurs.

"Good. I figured it would be fun to bring your fantasy to life." I grin up at him.

Snuggling as closely as I can, I drape my thigh over his and my arm over his stomach. My head rests on his chest and Steele tightens his arms around me. I swear I've never felt safer than I do at this moment.

"Thank you for trusting me enough to come to me," he whispers a few minutes later.

"There was no one else I even contemplated running to."

"What do you think about us having a little cookout this weekend? We'll invite everyone from Ink It Up and their families. I think it would be nice for you to get to know the people I consider my family a little bit better."

"I'd love that." I kiss him on the cheek, then snuggle back into his arms. "Thank you for making me feel like I belong in your life."

"It's easy when you fit in perfectly."

Chapter 16
Steele

As soon as the sun is streaming through the windows, I climb out of bed, careful not to wake Hannah up. It's a little harder since I have to hop to the bathroom and get my liner before I can put on my prosthesis, but I'm learning Hannah will sleep through almost anything, including alarms.

I tug on a pair of jeans and nothing else. After she gave me my fantasy two nights ago, I want to bring hers to life too. I'd love to walk around in just a pair of boxers, but I honestly don't like seeing my prosthesis. Just like Hannah's bruises, my prosthesis is a reminder of how I almost died. How I fought an uphill battle to get back to a normal life.

I wear long pants whenever I can so others don't have to see it. I don't want their pity or their sympathy. I've learned to deal with my disability and make sure it doesn't affect my ability to live life the way I want to.

From the letters we've sent each other over the years, I know Hannah's obsessed with pumpkin everything, especially pumpkin pancakes. I told her I had to run to the grocery store last night just so I could pick up the ingredients to make her pancakes this morning.

While I'm mixing up the batter, I turn the stove on low and wait for the skillet to heat up. I take a small measuring cup and pour the batter onto the pan.

I'm just placing the third pancake on a plate when Hannah stumbles into the kitchen. She's rubbing her eyes and looking for coffee. She's definitely not a morning person.

"Hey, what are you doing? I woke up and you weren't in bed."

"I'm making you breakfast." I grin.

She eyes me and moves a little closer, trying to see what I'm making. Once I have the next pancake cooking, I spin around and grab Hannah. I lift her onto the counter and step between her legs.

"Pumpkin pancakes," I say as I push a strand of hair behind her ear that fell out of her ponytail.

"Really? You remembered?" She wraps her arms around my neck and leans into me.

"Of course I remembered."

"You're going to make the perfect boyfriend for a lucky woman one day," she whispers.

"How about today?"

"Huh?" Her brows tug together and she stares at me in confusion.

"How about I make the perfect boyfriend for a lucky woman today? Be my girlfriend, Hannah Banana."

"I'd love to be your girlfriend." She presses a quick kiss to my lips, making me groan when she pulls away too fast for my liking. "Can we make a rule that you're only allowed to wear jeans and no shirt when we're home?"

"Fine, but only if the same rules apply to you." I grin.

"Steele! No! What if your friends pop in? I could totally see Rocco just walking in without knocking."

"Oh, he totally will. Somehow, he has a key to my house. I've changed the lock three or four times, and each time he somehow gets a new one. I don't know how to keep him out."

She laughs and shakes her head. "I can see Rocco being sneaky like that. I like him though. He's really funny and he seems like a great friend."

"He really is, but if you tell him I said that I'll deny it until my dying breath."

"Why are you so mean to him?" She playfully swats at my chest.

"I don't know. It's just how our relationship has always been." I shrug. "Every once in a while, we have a little heart to heart, but for the most part, we bust each other's balls. And Rocco's scared of me so I could do anything and he's not going to challenge me."

"I can understand that. If I didn't know you so well, I probably would've cried when I first met you."

"You did cry, Hannah Banana." I chuckle. "You threw yourself in my arms and sobbed."

"Yeah, but that was different," she mumbles as her cheeks heat with embarrassment and she drops her gaze to my chest. "I wasn't scared of you, I was just overwhelmed."

"Hey, look at me." I place my knuckles under her chin and guide her gaze back to mine. "I was just teasing you. I don't think you understand how honored I am that you came to me when you needed help. It meant a lot to me. That first night I held you in bed, I knew I was a goner. I had to figure out a way to make you mine, but I didn't want to push you after everything you've been through."

"Barry and I weren't together long. I think if it had been longer or our relationship had been more serious, then it would be affecting me more. We only hung out once or twice a week in the beginning. It was only a few months before he found the first note. And I kinda ghosted him after he hit me the first time. It was two weeks before he came to find me and that was the night he put me in the hospital."

"Did he ever hurt you during…" I trail off, unsure of how to ask my question.

"No. I wouldn't sleep with him. I wasn't ready." She shakes her head. "It doesn't matter what he did, Steele. You're not him and I know that. I have complete trust in you."

"You're making it so easy to fall for you," I murmur as I press my lips against hers.

A shrill alarm fills the air, making us jump apart. I glance around, trying to figure out what's causing the smoke alarm to go off.

"Fuck," I grumble as I snatch the pan off the stove and dump the pancake in the sink, then turn on the cold water.

I turn off the burner and place the pan on a cold one, then return to my place between Hannah's thighs.

"I'm sorry." Her eyes are filled with tears and she looks like she's moments away from falling apart.

"Sweetheart, you have nothing to be sorry for," I whisper, tugging her against my chest. I lift her off the counter and carry her over to the couch. I slowly lower myself to a sitting position, keeping her on my lap. "I burn shit all the time. That smoke alarm has gotten a workout since I bought this place."

"Really?" She pulls back and swipes under her eyes.

"Yup. The first time I had the guys over, I tried to make meatballs. I was an idiot and thought I'd put them on a baking rack so the grease would drip off... but I didn't think about putting a pan under them to actually catch the grease. My house filled with smoke while we were outside having a beer. When I came back inside it was so bad that I couldn't sleep here that night. So, a burnt pancake is nothing."

"You're a mess."

"I am. I need a beautiful woman to keep me in line." I grin at her. "Are you available to fill the position?"

"Yes, please."

"Good. Are you ready to eat? We have about forty minutes before we need to head to the shop."

"Definitely."

I carry Hannah back to the island and plant her on the counter. After I grab her plate and smoother her pancakes with syrup, I cut off a piece and raise it to her lips. She grins as she wraps her lips around the fork and pulls the pancakes off.

"These are amazing," she mumbles around her bite.

"Good. I've never made pumpkin pancakes before so I was afraid it was going to be a disaster, but I wanted to make something I knew you'd love."

I lift another bite to her mouth and a drop of syrup falls on her chest before she can eat it. Placing the fork on the plate, I lean in and lick the syrup off the swell of her breast.

"Holy shit," Hannah mumbles. "That was so sexy."

A laugh bubbles out of me and I shake my head. I never thought I could find someone perfect for me, but Hannah might be. I'm learning her filter doesn't work as much when it's just the two of us and I love it. She doesn't hide anything from me.

"Can I lick syrup off of your chest?" She wiggles her brows.

"I would say yes, but the hair makes it a little difficult." I motion to my hairy chest with a scowl. "I think we should stick with your chest."

"Sounds like a plan." She grabs the bottle of syrup and pushes me back enough for her to jump down. She intertwines our fingers and tugs me towards the bedroom.

"What are we doing?" I chuckle. She's way too excited for whatever she has planned.

"You'll see." She flashes me a wicked grin over her shoulder.

Fuck, I could get used to this.

I blow out a long breath as I lie naked on my bed. Hannah's next to me, trying to catch her breath too. After she poured syrup over her chest and I licked it off, things went a little further than I expected, but I'm not complaining. I loved every second of it and I'm probably going to beg for a repeat performance tonight.

"I think we need to get ready," Hannah groans.

"That's really hard when you're still naked in my bed."

"Oh, I'm sorry. I'll just leave." Hannah slides to the edge of the bed, but before she can get up, I wrap my arms around her waist and drag her back until she's lying across my chest. "AH! Steele!" She giggles and squirms around.

"Hannah Banana, if you keep squirming around on my lap, we're never getting out of this bed." I grind my hips against her and her eyes widen. I wrap my hand around the back of her neck and pull her in for a quick kiss before I let go of her. "Get that pretty little ass ready for work before we're late."

We pull into the parking lot of Ink It Up and I glance at Hannah's car. It's been here for a few days. Though Cole and Sammie haven't said a word about it, I feel like we should move it.

"Can we bring your car back to my house tonight?" I ask as I take Hannah's hand in mine.

"Yeah, I was thinking about that this morning." She stares at her car for a moment. "Hey, there's something on my windshield."

I release her hand and let her grab the paper. As she slowly walks back to me, her hands begin shaking as her eyes skim over the words.

"What's wrong, Hannah?"

"He... he found me," she whispers.

I scan the parking lot, looking for any evidence of someone watching us, but I don't see anyone.

"Let's get inside." I place my hand on her lower back and quickly lead her into the shop.

There's no one behind the desk, so I lift Hannah onto the stool and remove the paper from her hand.

You can't run away from me. I love you and I won't let him have you. You will be mine.

"Hannah," I breathe as I wrap my arms around her.

"How did Barry find me?" She whispers in disbelief. She's frozen, staring at the paper like it's going to come to life and try to grab her.

"I don't know, but you're not leaving my side until we find him."

The door opens and my head snaps to the side so I can see who's here. I don't trust Barry to stay away. Clearly, he's kept an eye on Hannah and we need to keep our guard up.

"Is everything ok?" Cole asks as he steps into the shop with Sammie and Knox behind him. The door is barely shut when Rocco and Damon walk through a few seconds later.

"What's going on?" Rocco asks as soon as he sees Hannah crying against my chest.

"Her ex found her and left a note on her car." I explain everything, knowing Hannah won't mind. She needs the support my friends can give her.

"I'm calling Mason. Him and Maddox can contact some of their friends who are still on the police force and I can have them start looking for Barry. Their private security and investigation company is doing really well. They're perfect for this job." Cole is already lifting his phone to his ear. His conversation with Mason is brief and ends with Mason saying he'll stop by the shop today to talk to Hannah.

"I can't afford that," Hannah pulls back to look at Cole as soon as he's off the phone. "I don't exactly have a job right now and I'm sure that would be expensive."

"Don't worry about that, sweetheart. I'll handle it." I shake my head. Her safety is much more important than money.

"Well, I might be able to help with that." Cole grips the back of his neck and glances around. "I was going to have to break this news today anyway."

"What's going on, Cole?" Damon asks, folding his arms across his chest.

"Ashley quit. She didn't give any notice. She called me late last night and said she wouldn't be back. I don't really know what's going on, she wouldn't talk to me."

"How does that help Hannah's situation?" Knox asks, mirroring Damon's position.

"We need someone to run the front of the shop. If Hannah wants the job, it's hers. This doesn't have to be a permanent thing if you don't want it to be, but it could be if you're interested."

"How is that a good idea? Hannah will be sitting up here by herself all day. What's stopping Barry from walking right in here?" Rocco frowns at Cole.

"Achilles," Knox says. "And I didn't tell anyone yet, but we just got another military dog. Patroclus' owner died while on duty and he was injured. It sounded similar to Achilles' story, and we jumped at the chance to adopt him. We could keep both of them behind the desk."

"Hold up. You got a dog named Patroclus? You know in Greek mythology Patroclus and Achilles were wartime companions, right?" Damon chuckles.

"Willow loved it. She thought Patroclus was destined to be ours." Knox smirks.

"I'm not letting Hannah sit up here when my cubby is the last one." I glare at them. "I'd rather pay for everything and have her sitting next to me so I know she's safe." I appreciate their ideas and willingness to help, but no. I'm not doing this.

"You can have my cubby. I'd love to be in the back." Damon shrugs.

"That's because then you could watch your camera feeds without anyone noticing." Rocco grins. "Last week he was checking the one in his bedroom when I came in. Shay was butt naked and I almost puked."

"Well, asshole, no one invited you into my cubby and you weren't forced to look over my shoulder." Damon rolls his eyes. "Shay's creeped out now."

"If you stopped creeping on her, she wouldn't have gotten peeked on. Cammie died laughing when I came home traumatized."

"Shay knew I was watching her and she loves it," Damon argues.

"What do you think?" I turn to Hannah, ignoring Damon and Rocco as they continue to fight with each other. I don't care if Rocco saw Shay's tits.

"I think I'd be ok with it if Achilles and Patroclus are at my feet and if you're right there." She points to Damon's cubby.

"I'll call Willow right now and have her bring the boys over."

Chapter 17
Hannah

Five minutes before the shop officially opens, a beautiful woman with chestnut hair and dark chocolate eyes holds the door for two huge dogs to enter before her.

"Hey, you must be Hannah." She smiles at me. "I'm Willow and this is Achilles and Patroclus." She motions to the dogs who immediately round to my side of the counter and lie down on a dog bed under the desk.

"Hey, baby. Thanks for bringing them." Knox kisses Willow, then places a protective hand on her rounded belly. "How are you feeling?"

"Good. Are you still planning on meeting me at the ultrasound?"

"Yes. I should be done with this tattoo by one, so being there by two is no problem. I'll leave Achilles and Patroclus here, then Steele said he'll drop them off to us on his way home."

"Are you sure you guys don't mind me stealing your dogs?" I glance down at the two laying at my feet.

"We don't mind at all," Willow says softly, then she glances at Knox. He nods his head, giving her permission for... something. "Achilles saved my life. He alerted me when my abusive father was outside of Knox's house and it gave me enough time to call Knox. He saved Knox's life by taking a bullet from my father for him. He's protected all of us at one time or another."

"Your dad abused you?" I swallow hard.

"Yup. Physically and emotionally. It was rough. Knox saved me from all of that. I knew he'd protect me from anything and that was the push I needed to leave."

"My mom physically abused me before she died from a heart attack," I whisper. "She's the reason I installed a second lock on my bedroom in my apartment. I think that's what kept Barry out the first time he hit me."

"My boys will keep you safe, I promise." Willow smiles sadly.

"The dogs or the guys?" I chuckle.

"Both." Her grin widens.

"Achilles and Patroclus will stay hidden unless they think there's a threat. If you feel uneasy, they'll pick up on that and be a little more on guard. Patroclus hasn't been here before, but he'll follow Achilles' lead. They're very in tune with each other already," Knox says softly.

"Ok, boys. I'm going home," Willow says a little louder. Achilles and Patroclus perk up and quickly move around to her. She squats down and wraps her arms around both of their necks as they cover her face with kisses. "You two be good and protect Hannah."

Their ears perk up when she says protect. I wonder how intense their training was and how much they understand.

As soon as Willow leaves, Knox tells the dogs to lay back down. They quickly obey and curl up on the large dog bed together.

"I think you can fit at least one more dog on here." I chuckle at how close they stay to each other.

"I'm telling you, if you didn't know better, you'd assume they've had each other their entire lives and not just a few weeks. It's crazy." Knox shakes his head with a grin. "I'm the second cubby, Hannah. I'll hear them if anything bothers them. Achilles, Patroclus, schützen." His voice is firm and demanding. The dogs look up at him like they completely understand before they relax again.

"What did you just tell them?"

"I instructed them to protect you. They know English, but they were trained in German. They know the command is more important if I say it in German." He shrugs a shoulder. "I'm right there, Hannah." He points to the second cubby. "Just call out if you need anything and you'll have all six of us running up here."

The morning goes smoothly. When a client needs to check out, the guys show me how to use the computer and how to charge them for their tattoos. It's a little easier because they only accept credit cards and no cash for the actual tattoos. We only accept cash for tips.

The computer is fairly easy to use and they have everything set up nicely. When a client comes in and I check them in, it starts a timer. They get charged per an hour and the program keeps track of how long it's been. We can manually adjust it, but most of the time we don't need to. When the client checks out, it adds up the cost of the tattoo automatically.

The door opens and an attractive man with broad shoulders and the most gorgeous gray eyes steps into the shop. He looks like he belongs in the military, he's basically a real-life G.I. Joe doll.

"Hey, are you Hannah?" He pushes his sunglasses to the top of his head.

"Yes?"

"I'm Mason. I'm friends with Cole and Sammie. The rest of the guys too, but I grew up with Cole." He shakes his head. "Sorry, it's been a long morning and my coffee hasn't kicked in yet."

"It's ok." I chuckle.

"Cole told me a little bit about what's going on, but I'd like to hear it from you."

"Hey, Mason. Thanks for coming, man." Steele exits his new cubby and shakes Mason's hand.

"Of course. I know how important our women are. Clearly, I'd do anything to protect mine." He shakes his head. "At least Hannah hasn't gotten herself kidnapped by sex traffickers."

"What!" My eyes widen as I stare at him in horror.

"Yeah, my Firefly made saving her difficult. Your situation is a walk in the park for me to handle. I just need more information on Barry like a last name, address, and where he works."

I spend the next thirty minutes talking to Mason and answering all of his questions. He's going to have his guys look for Barry. From what Cole has told me, it sounds like Mason and his men have been more successful in finding people than the police tend to be. That's a little more reassuring, but I know Barry. If he doesn't want to be found, he won't be.

I smile as the client says goodbye and walks out the door. We only have twenty minutes left before the shop technically closes for the night. Steele, Rocco, and Damon still have clients with them, but Sammie, Cole, and Knox are done for the day.

I busy myself with answering some questions on social media and trying to make some new graphics for some of the shop's social media. Ashley used to be in charge of Ink It Up's presence on social media, and I'm trying to make sure I'm taking over all of her jobs. I don't want Cole or Sammie to have to pick up any of the slack.

A low growl rumbles from below the counter and I freeze. When another growl mixes with the first, my hands start shaking. Achilles and Patroclus slowly stalk out from behind the counter and place themselves between me and the door.

"Steele!" I whimper as I stare out the door and try to figure out what has them on guard.

Steele's at my side a second later, ripping off his gloves and tossing them in the trash before he tugs me into his arms.

"What's going on?" Rocco and Damon join us a few seconds later.

"I don't know. Achilles and Patroclus started growling and moved around the counter. I don't know what has them on edge though."

"I'm locking the door. It's almost closing time and no one should be coming in here. We can unlock it when our clients need to leave." Damon turns the lock and drops the shades on the windows and doors. "I'm checking the back door, then finishing this tattoo."

"Go in Steele's cubby with him. You don't need to be out here. We can ring out our clients ourselves." Rocco puts a brotherly hand on my shoulder and squeezes gently before he disappears down the hall to his client.

"C'mon, sweetheart." Steele places a gentle hand on my lower back and leads me to his cubby. "Derek, do you mind if my girl and two dogs hang out in my cubby too?"

"Nah. The more the merrier."

"I wouldn't go that far. You'll end up with Rocco in here if he hears you." Steele chuckles.

"Willow told me about the new dog, but I haven't met him yet. Achilles is pretty badass though." Derek glances at me, seeing I'm confused on how he knows Willow. "I work with Willow at the hospital. Well, she actually works for me technically. I own the general surgery practice she works for."

"Oh, that's awesome." I smile.

"Achilles. Patroclus. Kommen." Steele's voice is strong and commanding. He's every bit of the scary ex-SEAL I know he can be.

The dogs respond instantly. They both enter the cubby, then spin around and sit in the doorway, keeping their attention on the front door of the shop.

They're not growling anymore, but their ears are perked and they're on high alert. I'm so thankful Willow brought them in today. They definitely made me feel safer.

"Hannah works in pre-op and post-op," Steele says as he turns his attention back to the tattoo.

"Really? If you ever want a job at Rosewood University Hospital, let me know. I'm sure between Willow, Kelsey, Cali, Jesse, and I, we could help you get one."

"Thanks, I'll keep that in mind. I'm still trying to figure out what my future looks like."

Steele's eyes meet mine and it feels like he's wordlessly begging me to stay. What he doesn't realize is I want to stay too.

Chapter 18
Steele

Achilles saw or heard something that's put him on edge. I know it. I've spent the last hour trying to act unaffected, but I know something is up. I'm not really sure what to do though. Until Barry makes a move, there isn't much I can do.

The second he tries to come near Hannah, he's fucking dead. The rest of the guys were fine with the idea of their girls' attackers going to jail, but I'm not. I want him six feet under.

I'm not going to let Hannah be scared for the rest of her life that Barry could get out and come after her again. I'll make sure to end her fear and worry once and for all.

"We're not taking Achilles and Patroclus to Knox. We're taking them home," I murmur as I lock up the door after Derek leaves.

"Won't they be upset about that?"

"No. They'll understand."

"Give me your keys." Rocco holds out his hand and I drop them into his open palm without a second thought.

"Why did he want your keys?" Hannah frowns at where he exited at the back of the shop.

"He's going to bring my car around to the back entrance of the shop. You'll be able to hop right in and we won't have to be in the open. Plus, if Barry sees him get in my car, he might not realize it's mine. Then, he might not follow us to my house. If he doesn't already know where I live, I'd rather keep it that way."

Hannah swallows hard and her hands shake at her side. She's terrified of him. I don't blame her. If he went crazy over a few letters, there's no telling what he'll do now that she's staying with me.

"I'm scared, Steele," she whispers.

"I know, sweetheart, but I won't let anything happen to you. I'll protect you until the day I die."

"That's not reassuring! What if he goes after you?"

"I'm pretty hard to kill. Tons of people have tried already and failed." I smirk, trying to lighten the situation, but it doesn't help.

Rocco does our secret knock, the one we've used since we were in the service, and I quickly open the door.

"I don't see anything strange, but I don't trust that. If Achilles says something is off, I believe him." Rocco drops my keys into my hand. "Do you want to jump in the back and I'll drive you guys home?"

"How will you get home then?" Hannah stares at him like he's crazy.

"I'll have Pit Bull come get me." He shrugs. "My car can stay here overnight in case the asshole's watching. I wouldn't want him to realize Steele's car isn't mine, or he'll know who to follow. I can have Pit Bull drive me to your house in the morning and I'll drive the two of you in again."

"No, you don't need to do that." Hannah waves him off.

"Yeah, let's do it," I say. "Anything to keep Hannah safer. I have a feeling he just found Hannah and if we can go home without him watching, I'd rather that."

Rocco snatches my keys out of my hand and exits the shop. This time he opens the back door of my SUV.

"Kommen, Achilles and Patroclus." Rocco motions for them to hop in the back before turning his attention back to us. "Let's go, beautiful."

Once we've climbed into the backseat, Achilles hops into the front passenger's seat and his gaze sweeps over everything. Patroclus mirrors his position from beside

Hannah. They're both more than on alert and that makes me uneasy.

Rocco cranks the engine and locks the doors. He slowly pulls out of the parking lot and heads in the opposite direction from my house.

"Where are we going?" Hannah asks nervously.

"We're not going straight home. We need to make sure no one is following us first," I explain calmly.

"I'm guessing this isn't the first time you've done this?"

"Sadly, no. We're pretty experienced with this shit. Every one of us fell in love with a woman with baggage in the form of a crazy man going after them." Rocco keeps his full attention on the road in front of him.

I trust him more than any other person behind the wheel. He was always the one driving when we were overseas. He saw things no one else did and because of that, we missed being killed more times than I can count. Rocco's amazing at making those split-second decisions too. He'd catch movement on the side of the road and instantly throw a U-turn. Later we'd find out there was a group of terrorists waiting to gun down our vehicle. If it weren't for Rocco, I would've died at least a dozen times while we were deployed. I owe him everything. Especially after he saved my life after the accident.

"There's a car following me." Rocco's voice is void of emotion. "He's good, I'll give him that much. He's kept two cars between us the entire time, but he's not as good as I am." He grips the steering wheel so hard his knuckles are turning white.

Hannah tightens her hold on my hand and lets out a quiet whimper. She's terrified, but I'll never let him get to her again.

"It's ok, Hannah Banana. Rocco will lose him, then we'll be safe at home. I'm betting he saw us park this morning and he knows this is my car. He's not positive you're in here, but he's hoping you are." I try to reassure her as I wrap my arms around her to make her feel at least slightly safer.

"Hannah, the guys helped me protect Pit Bull. We helped Damon protect Shay and Max, and we helped Knox protect Willow. We're not going to sit by and let this asshole get to you. There isn't a better group of men to protect you. Hell, I almost died after that piece of shit went after Pit Bull, but I made sure to protect her in the process. Steele and Knox had to save my life and I'm not sure Knox was happy about it, but I made it." Rocco shrugs.

"What if he comes after you and tries to kill you? He said he wasn't going to let you have me," Hannah cries.

"Stop, Roc. You're not making this better."

"All I'm saying is, Steele killed someone to protect my girl. None of us will hesitate to kill Barry if it comes to that."

"You killed someone?" Hannah stares up at me with wide eyes.

"Sweetheart, I've killed plenty of people in my life. Everyone except Cammie's stalker was when I was in the military. But this asshole tried to kill my best friend and then he tried to go after Cammie. I wasn't risking him coming back again. So, I'm serious when I say I'll do whatever it takes to keep you safe."

Hannah settles back into my arms and breathes out a long breath. I can only imagine what's going through her head right now. She's probably terrified. Hell, I'm scared and I know I can hold my own against this guy, especially with Rocco at my back.

"Hold on, guys." Rocco presses hard on the gas and we race through an intersection as the light turns red.

I glance over my shoulder and see Barry's car. He's trying to get around the cars in front of him, but there's no way for him to do it.

We take a left, then a right. Rocco zig zags his way through our town and takes a solid fifteen minutes to get to my house when it should've been three. He pulls straight into the garage and quickly shuts the door before anyone can drive by and see that my car is in here.

"Are you doing ok, Hannah?" He spins in his seat to face her.

"Are you sure he didn't follow us here?" She nibbles on her bottom lip, looking seconds away from crying.

"I promise. We lost him when I went through that red light, but I made sure he was nowhere to be seen before I turned into the development."

"Sweetheart, we can go into the house through the garage. There's no way for him to know we're home, even if he knows where I live."

"I can stay the night if you want. I just need to call Cammie and let her know what's going on."

"No, you need to get home to your family. I don't trust Barry, but I wouldn't want Cammie and Lana home without you the entire night." Hannah quickly brushes off his concern.

"I'm not so worried about my wife." Rocco chuckles. "After her stalker, she took a bunch of different martial arts classes and she has guns hidden all over the house. She says she's never going to be vulnerable again. Honestly, if Barry got into my house, I'd be more worried about him than

Cammie or Lana. No one comes between a mama bear and her cub, and lives to tell about it."

"We'll be alright, Roc. You know I'll call you if anything comes up." I open the back door and help Hannah out of the seat. She doesn't move more than a few inches away from me as we wait for Achilles and Patroclus to jump down. "Let's sweep the house just to be safe."

"Of course."

Rocco slips a key out of his pocket and unlocks my door, not the one from my key ring, but one from his own. I don't bother saying a word. Maybe it's better if he can get in here, especially with Barry lurking around.

He walks straight into my kitchen and grabs a gun from a hidden drawer, before checking one room after another. I grab another gun hidden on top of a bookshelf and follow him after I tell Hannah to stay in the living room with the dogs.

"He's going to find her," Rocco whispers when we end up in my room.

"Yeah, I know." I run a rough hand through my hair and let out a long sigh.

"If he was able to figure out where she was, there's no way he won't figure out where you live. Hell, are you sure he didn't find an envelope from one of your letters and already knows where you live?"

"No. The fucker probably does, but I don't want Hannah freaking out."

"If he comes sniffing around your house, you guys can stay at our house."

"I'm not putting Cammie and Lana in jeopardy. I'm not going to put Shay and Max or Willow and the baby in jeopardy either. We need to stay here."

"Are your cameras up and working?" Rocco arches a brow.

After Willow's attack, I thought about getting security cameras. Then when Max's uncle tried to kidnap him, security cameras seemed like an even better idea. But Cammie's stalker was the one that convinced me to buy them.

"Yeah. I don't check them often, but they're working."

"Good. Check the feeds since Hannah showed up. See if anyone's been lurking around your house or if any weird cars have driven by. We know he's driving a blue Chevy Impala."

"I will. Thank you for driving us. Is Cammie coming?"

"Yeah, she wants to meet Hannah though."

"Of course she does." I roll my eyes, but I'm not annoyed. How can you get annoyed with friends who care this much?

Chapter 19
Hannah

A beautiful woman with blonde hair and brown eyes comes bouncing into the living room with an adorable little girl on her hip. She stands on her tiptoes to press a kiss to Rocco's lips before handing off the baby.

"Hi! I'm Cammie." She smiles in my direction.

"Her name is Pit Bull." Rocco rolls his eyes.

"Hey, Cams. How are you?" Steele wraps her in a tight hug before letting her go and snaking an arm around my waist.

"I'm doing well. We all are." Cammie turns her attention back to me. "But that's not important. I'm here to meet the woman who stole Steele's heart. It's so nice to meet you, Hannah."

"You too." I try to smile, but it's forced. I'm still scared of Barry showing up and now that Cammie and Lana are here, I'm even more nervous. I don't want them to get caught in the crosshairs and get hurt.

"I think Hannah's a little overwhelmed right now, babe." Rocco places his arm around her waist and tugs her into his chest. "We should go and give them a chance to relax."

"But I didn't even get to talk to Hannah." She sticks her bottom lip out into a pout.

"I'm sure this isn't the only time you'll meet her. Hell, I don't think Steele's going to let her leave." Rocco chuckles.

"Not a chance," Steele growls.

"Fine, but I expect us to get together soon." Cammie points at Steele with a raised brow.

"We will. Hannah and I were talking about having a BBQ and inviting all of Ink It Up and their families."

"Oh! Quinn and the guys invited all of us to a BBQ at the cabin next weekend. That could be a nice little getaway and a way to put some distance between you and your ex."

Lana lets out a little whimper and Rocco peppers her cheeks with kisses. She giggles and pushes against his face, but she's loving it.

"C'mon, babe. She's getting tired. You know if she falls asleep on the way home, she'll never sleep through the night tonight." Rocco places his hand on Cammie's lower back and guides her towards the door.

"Fine. It was nice to meet you, Hannah!" She calls over her shoulder as they exit the house.

Steele locks the door before moving around the house and checking again to make sure all the windows are secured. He grabs a tablet from on his desk in the living room and clicks around until multiple camera feeds fill the screen.

"Let's go to bed, baby." Steele holds out his hand to me and I take it happily.

We stayed at the shop later today. Thursdays, Steele always works later in the day so we got takeout for dinner and ate between his appointments. I've never been so thankful for that. The idea of making dinner or having to go out to get something makes me nauseous. Hell, I don't even think I could eat right now.

Steele places his tablet on the nightstand, before heading into the bathroom. He takes off his prosthesis in there, which is odd. He quickly rinses off his liner, but this time he dries it and brings both the liner and the prosthesis back into the bedroom. He places them next to the bed and then climbs in.

The tablet is in his hands seconds later. His full attention is focused on whatever is on the screen.

"What's going on, Steele?" I ask cautiously. I'm not sure I really want to know.

"I'm checking my camera feeds. I need to figure out if Barry knows where I live. Were any of the envelopes from my letters left lying around your apartment?"

"No. I always threw out the envelopes and put the letters into a box. And the envelopes were always trashed before Barry came over. Unless he went through my trash, which I think I would've noticed, he couldn't have gotten your address from that."

"You keep my letters in a box?" Steele arches a brow and a slow smile spreads over his lips.

"Yes. Don't judge me." I fold my arms over my chest and drop my attention to his chest.

"Hannah Banana, open the bottom drawer of the nightstand on your side of the bed."

I do as he says and a grin lifts the corners of my lips. He keeps my letters too. I riffle through them, trying to see how far back he has. I frown when I only find about six months' worth of letters.

"The drawer only holds so many." He chuckles. "The rest are in a box in my closet."

"You have all of them?" My attention snaps to him and I find amusement filling his features.

"Of course I have all of them. Even back to the very first one you wrote. And since you were kind enough to date each letter, they're in chronological order." He smirks.

"You never dated yours, so I did it myself and put the date I received on them," I huff.

"Damn, do you realize our entire relationship up until last week is written on paper and we have the complete set? How many couples can say that?"

"When we don't have to worry about Barry anymore, maybe we could read a few every night before bed."

"I love that idea… I'm fairly certain it will take us months, if not years, though." He grips the back of his neck.

"I don't have any plans." I nibble on my bottom lip, unsure if he truly wants me to stay here.

"You have no clue how happy the thought of you staying with me forever makes me." Steele reaches out a hand to me and tugs me until I climb back in bed with him.

"So, what are we looking for?" I rest my head on his chest and watch the feeds playing out on the tablet.

"Any sign of Barry walking by or a car driving slowly past my house. I started the night you showed up here, and I'm going to go through the footage until today."

"That's going to take forever!"

"I don't care, sweetheart. You're all that matters to me." He presses a soft kiss to my temple before turning his attention back to the screen.

After two hours of watching various people walk their dogs and hundreds of cars drive past Steele's house, I start to drift off to sleep. I'm exhausted after all of the adrenaline pumping through my body today.

"Motherfucker," Steele growls, startling me awake.

"What's going on?"

"He's been watching us for a few days. He knows where I live and after we left for work on Tuesday, he came looking in my windows." Steele scrubs a hand down his face and lets out a long breath.

"What do we do?"

"We act like we're unaware. Achilles and Patroclus are laying on the floor at the foot of the bed. You saw how well trained they are. If anything seems out of the ordinary, they're going to notice and alert us."

He leans over and tugs open the top drawer of his nightstand. He pulls out a gun and lays it on top.

"Do you know how to shoot a gun?"

"I've done it a few times, but not regularly." I lift a shoulder in a shrug.

"Well, you know which end to point at the bad guy, right?" He smirks and I roll my eyes.

"Yes."

"There's another gun in your nightstand. They're both loaded and ready to be used."

"Don't you worry about someone getting hurt?"

"Hannah, who's going to get hurt? I live alone. Last time I checked, I knew how to safely handle a gun."

"I don't know! Lana or Max?"

"They don't come over here, and if they did, I'd find somewhere safe to keep the guns until they left. I don't have kids living here and it's easier for everyone if I come to them. The kids have their own toys at their houses. Plus, there are highchairs and cribs. It's too much of an inconvenience for them to come here. We always hang out at Damon's or Rocco's houses now. I'm sure once Willow has the baby, we'll be hanging out there for a while because infants are even more work and need more things."

"I guess that's true."

"I'm going to text the guys and let them know what's going on, then we're going to try to get some sleep."

"Do you really expect me to be able to sleep now that I know Barry's been sniffing around here?" I stare up at him like he's crazy.

"I'll always protect you, Hannah. You don't need to be scared when I'm here." He presses another kiss to my temple and I blow out a long breath.

He's right. I know he'll protect me and I need to calm down. Nothing good can come from me losing sleep. I'll just be cranky and not pay attention to the world around me. Yeah, sleep is a good idea.

Chapter 20
Steele

Steele: Barry knows where I live. He was snooping in my windows two days ago.

Rocco: Motherfucker. What are we doing?

Damon: What do you think his plan is?

Knox: He's either going to try to kill one of you... maybe both of you *shrugging emoji* or he's going to kidnap Hannah.

Rocco: Wow, Knox. You're a fucking ray of sunshine, huh?

Knox: Pussyfooting around this isn't going to help. We need to be realistic. We didn't take Cammie's stalker seriously enough and he almost killed Rocco.

Damon: Aww, he cares about you Rocco. *heart emoji*

Rocco: What was the point of him following us if he knows where you live? That seems stupid and a little reckless.

Knox: He knows it will be easier to get to them in public. Especially if they separate. At home, he doesn't know what he's walking into. I don't think he's nearly as stupid as you all think he is.

Rocco: Another ray of sunshine. Shit, if you keep going, you'll put the sun to shame.

Steele: I think you're right. He's not being reckless. He's biding his time. I'm shocked he left the note on Hannah's car. Without that, we wouldn't be aware he was even here.

Knox: He wants her to be scared. He has power over her if she's scared.

Steele: So... what do I do?

Damon: He's not going to touch anyone at the shop or at your house. If he wanted to, he would've already done it. I think Knox is right. He's waiting for you to separate in public.

Steele: I repeat, what do I do?

Knox: You separate in public and draw him out. Mason and Maddox could have their team already in place. Damon and I probably could be there too. I doubt he's figured out who we are. Rocco needs to sit this one out though, he's seen you.

Rocco: Oh, c'mon! That's not fair!

Knox: You tried to die the last time.

Rocco: I didn't *try* and, in the end, I didn't die, so I don't really understand why this is being held against me. *frowning emoji*

Rocco: Plus, it was over a year ago. How long do we hold onto these things?

Knox: For as long as you're married to my sister.

Rocco: Would you really want me to leave Cammie? Could you imagine how pissed she'd be?

Damon: She'd stab Knox.

Steele: She'd stab everyone she thought planted the idea in Rocco's head.

Damon: She'd cry... a lot.

Steele: And break things.

Damon: And she wouldn't want to share Lana or Duke, so that would turn into a custody suit. Plus, the house was Rocco's before they got married so he'd easily get it in a divorce.

Steele: Damn, all those lawyer fees, plus she'd have to find a new house? I don't think she'd be able to afford that on her designing income. I guess she'd have to get a new job.

Rocco: *Eating popcorn gif*

Damon: She'd probably need to go back to school and get a degree. Who will watch Lana when she's taking classes and working her ass off to make ends meet?

Steele: Maybe she could stay in a group home for a while.

Knox: My sister isn't staying in a fucking group home.

Damon: Stripping would probably make her more money and faster.

Knox: She's not stripping either! What the fuck is wrong with you?

Steele: Prostitution could get her into some sticky situations, especially if her pimp is an ass.

Damon: Ha! I see what you did there *grinning emoji*

Steele: I aim to please... I guess Cammie would have to too, if she didn't have Rocco to support her.

Knox: I fucking hate all of you. I'm blocking your numbers.

Steele: But you'll be at the farmer's market on Saturday to catch this asshole, right?

Knox: Yes. Now, fuck off.

Knox has left the conversation

Damon: He's going to be such an ass tomorrow.

Steele: 100%

Rocco: I don't think I've ever been so entertained in my life. I'm buying the two of you lunch for the next week after that performance. For once, Knox is pissed beyond belief, and none of his anger is directed at me!

Rocco: Also, Cammie appreciated your sticky situation joke, Steele. And she says she appreciates Damon's confidence in her being able to make a good living stripping.

Rocco: I told her if she got implants, she'd make more. Now she's thinking about it. She says it's an insurance policy in case I leave her. This woman is crazy to think I'd ever leave her *rolling eyes emoji* especially if she got bigger tits. I mean c'mon. I'd need to play with those for at least a few years.

"Are you sure about this?" Hannah glances over at me.

"I know this is scary, but I don't think we have another choice." I take her hands in mine and stare deep into her green eyes. The gold flecks in them are glittering in this light, making her look even more beautiful.

I tuck a strand of chocolate brown hair behind Hannah's ear and cup her cheek. I hate seeing her so scared. I wish I could do more to take away some of the fear and anxiety.

"What if he hurts me?" She whispers, breaking my heart.

"Hannah Banana, I promise you, he won't hurt you. The guys will be standing by. They're already in place and they won't move unless I tell them to. By the end of tonight, I'll make sure Barry is a distant memory."

"Ok. What do I have to do? I know you told me, but can you do it again?"

I spend the next few minutes going over our plan. She nibbles on her bottom lips and I can see her brain spinning with all the ways this could go wrong. She doesn't realize I've been thinking of nothing else for the last forty hours.

"Alright. Let's get this over with," she grumbles as she pushes open her car door and climbs out.

I round the car and instantly reach for her hand. Intertwining our fingers, I keep my grip on her tight. I don't trust Barry one bit, but I know there are more than enough eyes on us.

We walk around the farmer's market for the next hour. Moving from one seller to the next, we pretend we actually give a shit about what they're selling. The entire time, I'm aware of someone watching us and I don't think it's one of my guys, but I don't want to look around and tip him off.

Hannah moves under a small tent to get away from the sun. The tables are filled with different kinds of homemade jams.

"How about you look here, while I go check out that homemade beer table over there?" I point to a booth a dozen spots down.

"Steele," she whimpers.

"You're going to be ok, sweetheart. I can see Mason, Maddox, Knox, and Damon from here. Hell, I saw Cole and a couple of his friends too. Mason called in as many reinforcements as he possibly could."

"Can you loop back around after he moves towards me?"

"I'll be back at your side as quickly as I can possibly be." I tug her into my arms and press a soft kiss to her forehead.

"Just pretend you're oblivious to the world around you and check out these delicious jams."

"That's easier said than done," she grumbles under her breath.

"Is that because jam is gross?" I pull back far enough to smirk down at her.

"Steele! Shh!" She swats at my chest and glances around to make sure none of the workers are paying attention.

"Are you going to be ok? I'm not leaving your side until I know you aren't going to freak out. You need to act like you don't know Barry's here."

"I'm terrified something will go wrong."

"I'll have one of Cole's friends move closer. Nate or Nick look like the type of people to shop for jams."

"What's that supposed to mean?" She stares up at me with amusement.

"I don't know. They're the boy next door type. The guys you want to bring home to meet your family. They don't look like they'll break someone in half."

"So, the opposite of you?" She grins.

"Exactly." I kiss the tip of her nose, then pull out my phone and fire off a text. Cole answers immediately. "Cole said Nate and Nick are on their way. They'll be right here with you so nothing will happen to you. They might look sweet, but I've seen both of them protect their women, you're safe with them, sweetheart."

"I love you."

"I love you too. You'll be back in my arms soon."

Chapter 21
Hannah

I blow out a long breath as Steele walks out of the booth and away from me. I can't believe I'm doing this. Wouldn't it be easier to involve the police?

Except every time the police try to arrest Barry, he spots them from a mile away and disappears before they can snatch him off the street.

The entire time we've been here, I've felt like someone was watching me. When Steele was by my side, I was able to ignore it because I knew he wouldn't let anything happen to me. Now, I feel every hair standing on end and goosebumps spreading across my skin.

"We're here, Hannah. Stay calm," a gentle voice says.

I glance up to find two attractive men pretending to look at jams. One is a little taller and has striking green eyes and brown hair. You can tell he's strong, but he's got nothing on Steele.

The other has dark rimmed glasses that somehow makes his pale gray eyes stand out even more. His light brown hair is styled to the side and he looks kind of like Captain America.

I don't answer them because I don't want Barry to think I know them. And I really don't know them. They're complete strangers to me. I simply smile and go back to searching for a jam I don't really want.

"It's about time he left you alone," a voice growls in my ear as hot, garlic breath fans over my cheek.

My entire body tenses. His growl makes me scared and nervous as to what he'll do next, unlike Steele's growl, which makes me smile and feel more loved and protected.

"You're coming with me," he continues, but he makes no move to touch me.

I'm sure he's trying to play nice so he doesn't draw any unwanted attention, but I want everyone's focus on me.

"No. I'm not." I keep my words short so I don't stutter over them and try to make sure my voice is strong and confident.

"Didn't you learn your lesson about disobeying me? Do I need to beat you a little harder this time? Maybe it's because you don't have any bruises to remind you who you belong to. I'll just need to make sure you have one or two at all times." He reaches for my hand, but I step away from him. I don't want to feel his skin against mine.

"Don't touch me," I whimper as my mind replays the way he abused me last time and the terror I felt that night.

"I don't think you're understanding me, Hannah. You're coming with me whether you like it or not."

This time he grabs my arm forcibly and tugs me out of the booth. I try to dig my heels into the grass, but he's too strong.

"Let go of me!" I try to yell, but my words come out as barely a whisper. What is wrong with me? I shouldn't be this scared of him! He can't do anything to me. Not this time.

The next few seconds all happen in a blur. One second, Barry's holding onto my arm in a death grip and the next, he's laying on the ground with his face pushed into the grass.

"Get the fuck off of me!" He roars, trying to thrash out of Mason's hold.

It's almost comical how much stronger Mason is than Barry. He looks like it's taking very little effort on his part to keep my ex at bay.

"Nah, I think I'll stay right here. Your fat ass makes a comfy seat." Mason rolls his eyes.

"You can't do this to me! I didn't do anything wrong!" Barry tries again, but Mason's already wrenching his hands behind his back and cuffing his wrists.

"You didn't do anything wrong? Seriously? That's your argument? You beat your ex and put her in the hospital. I have no doubt if no one stopped you, you would've killed her. Now that she's found a new life without you, you're trying to drag her back to the hell she lived in with you. It's funny how you only went after Hannah when Steele wasn't around. He said you didn't have the balls to stand up to him, I guess he was right."

Barry's face is turning the deepest shade of red I've ever seen on a human. I'm almost waiting for steam to come billowing out of his ears. I'm not sure if it's because of the physical struggle, or if he's mad over Mason calling him out for being scared of Steele.

I do know that this is when he tries to lash out and I'm a little afraid of what he's going to do now.

"I've got you, Hannah Banana." Steele wraps his arms around me and tugs me against him. I bury my face in his chest and he cradles the back of my head. "It's ok, sweetheart. He can't hurt you anymore."

"Yeah, I don't think so, asshole," Mason growls and Barry lets out a squeal of pain.

I glance over my shoulder at them to find Mason's knee dug into Barry's back. He's struggling to fight against Mason again, and he's getting nowhere.

"Excuse me, Hannah. Can I get a statement from you?"

I spin around to find Officer Richards standing behind me with his notepad out. He's not wearing a uniform and now that I realize it's him, I'm fairly certain I saw him earlier when we were walking around the farmer's market.

"Officer Richards, what are you doing here?"

"Mason and I are old friends. He called me and let me know what was going on today. Since I already have a warrant out for Barry's arrest, I figured it would be nice to see this case through and be here when he got arrested. The department agreed to let me come in street clothes and I got permission from Rosewood's police department to handle this."

We both glance at Barry as he roars with anger again and tries to flail his body around to get Mason off of him.

"Dude, just give up. He's not going to let you up," a cute man with dirty blonde hair and deep chocolate eyes says. He flashes me a lopsided grin and winks when he catches me watching him. He looks like he's more than trouble.

"Linc, keep your eyes off my girl," Steele growls. "And don't fucking wink at her."

"Down boy. I'm just trying to be nice. Jeez, I have a smoking hot wife. I'm not looking for anyone else." He rolls his eyes and turns to talk to Cole.

"Hannah, Mason said Barry's been stalking you. Is that true?"

"Yes. I have footage of him snooping around my house and he tried to follow us home from work one day," Steele says before I can respond.

"Can I have that footage? That would really help your case."

"Definitely. Anything to get that asshole locked up."

"Between the hospital records, your neighbor's statement – and he says the night you ended up in the hospital wasn't the first time this happened – and now the footage of him stalking you and Barry trying to abduct you, I believe we have a good case against him and I guarantee he'll be put in jail."

"Really? He won't be able to come near me again?"

"No. And if or when he gets out of prison, you can have a restraining order. I'm fully aware that doesn't actually protect you and it's just a piece of paper, but I have total confidence that Steele and his friends can protect you. If Barry's stupid enough to come near you, I'll fight to get him thrown back in prison."

"Thank you, Officer Richards." I smile as my eyes fill with tears. He's been so kind to me and I appreciate it so much.

"Of course. I'll keep you updated with everything. I'm sure Mason will be contacting me over it too." He chuckles. "That man is relentless. The Rosewood police department lost some good men when he and Maddox left the force." He shakes his head with a sad smile. "Well, you two should go enjoy the rest of your day while I transport Barry to his new home away from home."

I thank the officer again before he joins Mason and says something. Mason chuckles and quickly climbs off of Barry. He's still thrashing around on the ground. Richardson and Mason practically lift him off of the ground and to his feet.

As soon as Barry's gaze lands on Steele and me, his eyes narrow and his features turn murderous.

"I'll fucking kill you for this. You and your boy toy," he hisses.

"I dare you to try," Steele growls. "I'd love to practice some of my skills I learned in the SEALs again." He wraps a protective arm around my waist and makes sure Barry knows where he stands in my life.

Richardson tugs on Barry's arm until he finally starts following him away from us, but he keeps glancing over his shoulder at me.

"I'll never leave you alone, Hannah. Never!"

Chapter 22
Steele

It's been a week since we watched Richardson cart away Barry in handcuffs. It took Hannah a few days to calm down and stop looking over her shoulder. She's slowly getting comfortable in my life and in my home.

"Steele, could I clean out a shelf in your linen closet?" Hannah calls from the bathroom.

Instead of answering her, I push myself off of the bed and mosey into the bathroom with her. I snake an arm around her waist and press a soft kiss to her neck.

"Hannah Banana, are you going to keep living here?"

She pulls back and blinks up at me for several long seconds before she says a word.

"I can find a new place to live. I've probably outstayed my welcome here. I'm sorry."

She tries to step out of my arms, but I don't let her. She's clearly not understanding what I'm saying.

Lifting her into my arms, I place her on the vanity and step between her legs. I want to make sure she understands what I'm about to say.

"Nope. You're not walking away from me, sweetheart. I think you misunderstood my question. I'm not saying I want you to leave, because I don't. So, are you going to keep living here?"

"I'd like to," she whispers.

"Good. Then stop asking me if you can change things. I want you to stop viewing this house as mine and start viewing it as ours. You can move stuff wherever you want."

"I don't want you to get mad." She stares up at me with big innocent eyes. There's so much vulnerability in them.

"You know, even if you do something to make me mad, I'd never hurt you. I'll talk to you like an adult and work things out. If I don't like something, I'll tell you in a calm way."

"Ok," she says softly.

"If I ever raise my voice to you or say something that upsets you, I need you to call me out on it, sweetheart. I'm a growly person and sometimes I let my anger get the best of me, but I've never raised my hand to anyone and I'm not going to start with you."

"Thank you." She sits up a little straighter and loops her hands around the back of my neck to pull me in for a kiss.

"Don't thank me for treating you the way you deserve to be treated," I murmur against her lips.

"Fine, I'll thank you for treating me better than anyone else ever has."

"Let me show you just how well I can treat you." I smirk and lift her into the air.

Hannah let's out a little squeal and wraps her legs around my waist. She buries her face in the crook of my neck and giggles. The sound wraps around me like a warm hug and I know she's the woman for me. The one I want to spend the rest of my life with.

It's crazy to think we only met in person less than a month ago. Some people would say we're moving too fast, but our relationship began ten years ago. We've spent an entire decade getting to know each other and meeting Hannah in the flesh only made me fall even harder for her.

"Where are you taking me?"

"To bed." I place her in the center of the mattress and stare down at her. "Where else do you think I'm going to worship this amazing body?" I grin as I grip the waistband of her pants and tug them down her legs, taking her panties with them.

"Damn, look at that smile," Rocco calls as soon as we arrive at the cabin.

The members of Operation Riot bought this cabin when they first became famous. They wanted a place they could escape from the world. Since then, they've bought each property as it's gone on the market. Now they own all ten cabins and don't have any neighbors around them for miles.

"Someone looks like they just got fucked." Rocco grins.

"Rocco! Don't be so crude!" Cammie swats at his chest. "Please, ignore him. The rest of us do."

"Oh, c'mon. If she can't handle me, how do you think she'll deal with Tyson and Cal all weekend?" Rocco folds his arms over his chest and glares at Cammie.

"Don't rope me into this. I get in enough trouble all by myself!" Tyson glares at Rocco.

"I'm a perfect angel. I have my Bailey and my babies, I don't care about anything else." Calan waves off Rocco's comment and positions himself behind Bailey. He has one arm around her waist with his hand resting on her round stomach and the other arm is holding one of his kids.

I lead Hannah through the patio and into the house. I think I'm going to need at least a few drinks in me before I can tolerate Tyson, Calan, and Rocco in the same place at the same time.

"I think you're going to want at least three of these before we go back out there." I hold a bottle of beer out to Hannah.

"They're not bad at all." She chuckles. "Try working in the medical field. Everyone has a perverted mind and none of them give a shit. They say whatever is on their mind all the time. These guys don't bother me. Especially Rocco. I like him. I think he's a sweet friend who truly cares about you."

"Aww, shit. Now he's going to beat me up since you just confessed your undying love for me." Rocco's voice comes from behind me and I roll my eyes, making Hannah laugh.

"Undying tolerance of you." Hannah raises a brow and points in his direction.

"You wound me, woman! I thought you were on my side!" Rocco grabs his chest in mock horror.

"Oh yes, babe. Everyone loves you. Every man wishes they were you and every woman wishes they could be with you." Cammie walks into the kitchen with Lana on her hip and she rolls her eyes.

"You don't need to be mean. You could simply say to stop screwing with Steele." He sticks out his bottom lip in a pout.

"Yeah, please tell him that, Cams," I practically beg.

"What's the point? He wouldn't listen anyway."

"Steele, could you hold Lana for a few minutes?" Rocco plucks the baby out of Cammie's arms and deposits her into my arms before I even respond. "I think I need to take my wife upstairs and spank her for sassing me."

He lifts Cammie over his shoulder and smacks her ass. She laughs loudly and swats at Rocco's ass too. He races off towards the bedrooms with her still slung over his shoulder.

"Well, I think you might be a big sister soon, Lana. Are you excited for that?" I coo at the adorable baby in my arms.

"You're adorable with babies." Hannah reaches out a hand and brushes Lana's hair off her forehead.

"Do you want kids?" I eye her.

"Definitely. I just never thought I'd find someone I was willing to have kids with." She shrugs.

"And now?" I arch a brow.

"I think I found the perfect man now." She grins.

Chapter 23
Hannah

Steele's making me fall in love with him even more. The way he's so gentle with Lana is making me wish I could have a baby with him right away.

"Ba-da-ba," Lana babbles and tries to stick her finger in Steele's mouth. He pretends to bite her, making her toss her head back and giggle.

He doesn't get disgusted by her drool covered fingers or how she's spread drool all over his cheek now. He doesn't care that she's slapped him three times in the last two minutes by accident. He's too busy smiling and enjoying his time with her.

"I see you got stuck with the baby." Calan chuckles. "Rocco's been trying to pawn her off on someone since he got here. He's determined to get Cammie knocked up again."

"Is he trying to keep up with you?" Steele arches a brow.

"No one can keep up with me." He smirks.

"And I'm not stuck with little Lana. I've been telling Rocco I'd come babysit for weeks and he hasn't called me. I love this little girl." He kisses her cheek and she giggles even louder.

"You better keep your legs shut or this one will have you knocked up in no time." A beautiful woman with a big round stomach kisses Steele on the cheek before tucking herself into Calan's side. "I'm Bailey. I belong to this one." She pokes Calan in the chest and grins up at him.

"Damn straight, baby. You're all mine."

"It's nice to meet you. I'm Hannah. I sort of belong to Steele." I peek up at him.

"She one hundred percent belongs to me," Steele says in a baby voice, making Lana flash him a sleepy smile. "When's Tyson going to have a kid? Or Quinn?" Steele asks as he softly sways Lana in his arms. She looks like she's going to fall asleep soon.

"Sasha's pregnant, but she isn't very far along... I actually don't know if I was supposed to tell anyone outside of the band so let's keep that on the down low." Cal grips the back of his neck and grimaces.

"Our lips are sealed," I promise. I know Steele would never spread that kind of news without permission.

"Quinn and Casey... I'm not sure if they've even thought about kids yet. Casey's trying to open her own entertainment law firm."

"That's a lot of work. I couldn't imagine trying to do that." I shake my head.

"Yeah, but she knows she'll automatically have four clients, so that makes it a little easier. There's an up and coming band we've been taking under our wing too. We've been talking about opening our own record label and production company so we could help other bands reach their goals in life without screwing them over like so many record labels do."

"I'm proud of how far the four of you have come. You can truly do whatever you want at this stage in your career." Steele nods his head in approval. "Sweetheart, would you mind grabbing that blanket from the diaper bag on the couch? It's Lana's and I don't want her to get cold. She likes to be warm when she's sleeping."

I glance up to find Lana's face nestled into the crook of Steele's neck. She's snoring softly and she looks so tiny in his arms. He's still rocking back and forth like a seasoned father and I find it absolutely sexy.

I want to be the woman who makes him a daddy. I want to know my children are going to be loved beyond belief and know they'll always be protected from the bad people of the world.

After I grab the blanket, I follow Steele outside. We settle into comfortable chairs on the deck and he introduces me to the rest of the people I haven't met yet.

"Unkie Steele!" A little boy rushes over to us and holds his arms up for Steele. I expect him to tell the little guy he can't hold him, but I'm shocked when Steele sweeps him into his free arm.

"We have to be quiet because baby Lana is sleeping," he whispers softly.

"I seep too?" The boy stares up at him.

"You can sleep on me if you want to, Max, but you don't have to."

"I want!" He lays his head on Steele's chest and places a hand on Lana's back. I can tell the two of them are pretty close, even with their age differences.

"Maxy, Uncle Steele is already holding Lana, how about I hold you?" Shay, who I've met in passing at the shop, grins down at her son. She's married to Damon and the two of them are adorable together.

"No, me like Unkie Steele." Max sticks out his bottom lip in a pout.

"He's fine, Shay. I don't mind at all. Does he want a blanket? I don't think Lana's is big enough for both of them."

"Do you want me to take Lana?" I ask quietly.

"Nah, I want to get all the baby snuggles I can this weekend. Plus, she'll wake up if she's moved."

Shay drapes a blanket over Max and he snuggles even deeper into Steele's chest. I swear my heart is going to burst out of my chest with love for this man.

"Dang, Steele. You're going to get Hannah pregnant with the way she's staring at you." Knox settles into a chair across from us. "I don't think I've ever seen such big heart eyes."

Steele glances over at me with a grin tugging on the corner of his lips. "It's all part of my master plan to get her to fall so deeply in love with me that she'll never want to leave."

"Mission accomplished. I'm already there." I grin back at him.

Chapter 24
Steele

"Are you sure you don't want Bret Michaels' name on your ass anymore?" I arch a brow. I'm not even trying to hide my amusement.

"I'm positive." Hannah folds her arms over her chest and glares at me.

"I'd like to hear this story."

"I had a thing for 80's hair bands. In college, my roommate scored tickets to see Poison and I got a little drunk at the concert. We ended up getting tattoos on our way home from it. I woke up the next morning and didn't remember anything. I found out about the tattoo when I was trying to get dressed and I was in pain."

"Why did you never tell me about this?" I motion for her to lay down on the table.

"Because it's embarrassing!"

"That you're in love with Bret Michaels or that you got his name tattooed on your ass?"

"First off, I'm not in *love* with him, he was just my favorite band member. Second, I can't be held responsible for my actions that night. Alcohol was involved and a great deal of it." She points a finger in my face.

"Damn, I wonder what I could get you to do if I supplied you with a great deal of alcohol." I smirk as I tug her pants down her legs.

"You? I'm fairly certain you could get me to do a lot without a drop of alcohol, so I'm a little worried what I might agree to under the influence." Hannah grimaces.

I run my hands over her bare skin and try to decide how I want to do her tattoo. Hannah didn't want to see the design I have in mind. She says she trusts me enough to tattoo whatever I want on her. I'm not sure if she's crazy, or if she really believes in me that much.

I don't think I could give someone else that sort of control over something that will be stuck on my body for the rest of my life, but I guess anything is better than the tattoo she currently has.

"You're positive you don't want to see the design?" I watch her carefully. If there's any sort of hesitation, I'm stopping and we can do this another time. Or she could just look at the damn design.

"Nope. I trust you." She waves a hand in the air, dismissing my concerns.

"Okay..." I clean off her skin, then carefully lay the stencil on. I want to make sure it's absolutely perfect. I'd hate to give her a tattoo that isn't the best it can possibly be.

Tugging off the stencil paper, I tilt my head to one side, then the other. I check every inch of it before I decide it's placed the way I want it.

"Are you ready?" I ask as I slip on a pair of gloves.

"Yup!" She nods her head. "Oh! I brought some of our first letters. I thought I could read them while you tattooed me."

"Really?" A slow smile spreads over my face as she glances over her shoulder at me.

"Yeah, is that ok? I thought it would be fun to relive the beginning of our relationship."

"I love that idea, sweetheart."

I place the needle of my tattoo gun into the ink and draw some up. Then I position my hand over her thigh and take a deep breath. I don't like knowing I'm going to cause her pain, but it's necessary if she wants this covered.

"*Dear Steele,*

I hope you don't mind me writing to you. I thought it would be fun for us to keep in contact with each other while you're overseas and serving our country. I appreciate the years of your life you're spending defending our freedoms. This world would be a much different place without people like you.

My name is Hannah Foley. I'm a freshman in college and I think I want to be a nurse. I debated on joining the military and doing nursing through there, but boot camp didn't seem appealing to me. I mean who wants to be yelled at and told to work harder? I can work plenty hard without someone in my face, telling me to go harder and faster, thank you very much.

Was boot camp awful? Wait... is it even boot camp when you're in the SEALs? I heard not a lot of people pass the SEALs boot camp, but I'm not sure if that's true or not.

I'm looking forward to hearing from you. Have a great day and stay safe.

Hannah."

"I remember when I received that letter." I smile down at her skin. "I was terrified of getting attached to you and then you abandoning me. I didn't even want to write you back, but I didn't want you to get upset or think I died or something."

"I know. Looking back, I wish I had known so I could've reassured you I wasn't going anywhere."

"Eh, I wouldn't have believed you."

She giggles before she drops the letter on a chair and picks up the next one.

"*Dear Hannah,*

Thanks for writing to me. I'm not sure where you got my contact information from, but I don't mind receiving letters.

I think it was a smart move for you to go to college instead of joining the military. When you're surrounded by this many men and barely any women, it can get overwhelming for the women.

The SEALs training is over a year long and more than 70% of people fail within the first month. It is the hardest thing I've ever accomplished. I don't think I would've survived without Rocco, Damon, and Knox by my side.

Steele."

"Ugh, I sounded like such an ass," I groan.

"You did not!" She laughs. "You were being cautious about opening yourself up to me. I like that about you."

I pause my work and glance up at her. She can't be serious right now. Everyone's always hated how long it takes to get me to allow someone to get close. Most people give up too quickly to ever make it.

"Why?" I ask slowly.

"Because I know what we have is real. I know you're not going to change your mind about us and you're definitely not going to push me aside for some random woman you meet. And when you let people in, you love them with everything you have. I appreciate that because I feel the same way."

"I love you, Hannah Banana."

"I know you do, and I love you, Steele."

"Why don't I have a nickname?" I grin.

"I could call you... Steely or Man of Steele."

"Please call me Man of Steele in front of Rocco. He'd get so mad." I chuckle. "Now, read me letters so I can get this tattoo done."

I lean down and kiss her ass cheek on the side I'm not working on. She laughs and grabs the next letter.

Dear Steele,

I'm so happy you responded! I wasn't sure if you would and I was feeling a little rejected until your letter showed up in my mailbox.

Yeah, I don't think I'd survive that. There's no way. You must be insanely strong mentally and physically. I could really use someone like you in my life. Maybe we should be best friends. I need someone to teach me to be stronger. Someone I know will always have my back. Are you up for the job?

Hannah."

"That letter made me want to let you in," I confess quietly. "I knew something was wrong in your life and I wanted to be the one to fix it. I wanted to protect you and be the strength you needed."

"You were exactly what I needed. You still are," Hannah whispers.

I rub my hand up and down her thigh, silently letting her know I'm never going anywhere. I'm here for the long run. She's all mine.

"*Dear Hannah,*

I can always be someone you can lean on when you need me. I guarantee you're stronger than you think. Most people don't realize the strength that lives inside of them until they're forced to use it.

You said you're in college and going to be a nurse, right? What do you want to be when you grow up? Do you want to work in the emergency room? The intensive care unit? The operating room?

As far as best friends go, I have three guys who are like brothers to me, but I don't see why I can't add a fourth best friend. I'm sure you could take them in a fight and get to the number one position.

Steele."

"I think you did a good job at getting to the number one position." I grin.

"I cried when I got this letter," Hannah admits softly.

"Why?" I frown down at where I'm working on her tattoo. I'm going to make sure this is the best cover up I've ever done.

"Because I needed to hear someone tell me I was strong and that I could lean on them. Then you showed interest in my life and offered me a place in yours. I'm fairly certain I read this letter at least a hundred times from the time I got it, until you sent the next one."

"That's adorable, sweetheart."

"Do you know I never considered working in the operating room until after you asked about it? You're the reason I started working in pre-op and post-op."

"I'm not sure if that's good or bad considering your work history." I frown, making her laugh, but she doesn't respond to that.

"*Dear Steele,*

When I wrote my first letter to you, I wasn't sure I was comfortable writing to a complete stranger. It was out of my comfort zone, but I needed a change in my life. I figured talking to someone on a different continent was a good place to start. It felt safer.

I'm so glad I took that chance. You have no idea how much your last letter meant to me. It's exactly what I needed to hear right now.

I'm still thinking I want to be a nurse when I grow up, but I don't know! What if I suck at it? What if someone pukes on me? I'm not sure I can handle that. Maybe I should revisit my college website and see what other majors I could choose. Maybe I should be a writer or journalist. I'm sure their chances of being puked on are pretty low.

Help me, Steele! I need someone else to make this decision for me. I trust your opinion.

Hannah."

"You trusted me pretty early." I chuckle.

"You seemed like a no bull-shit type of person." She lifts her shoulder in a shrug. "I don't know. You just seemed like someone who doesn't trust others easily and the fact that you were slowly letting me in made me feel like trusting you was the right thing to do."

"It was the best decision you've ever made." I grin at her.

"Dear Hannah,

I'm glad you took that chance too. I look forward to your letters more than I'm willing to admit, but I'm still not sure I can let you in completely.

Everyone leaves, Hannah. At the end of the day, no one sticks around. Not really. I'm not sure I can let you in, knowing you're going to leave.

I think you're going to be a great nurse. If you didn't care about other people, you never would've began writing to me. You're easy to talk to and have a way of calming me and helping me escape my shitty reality for a little bit.

If you ever meet my friend Rocco, stay far away from him. He's already talking about dating you and trust me, sweetheart, Rocco Reeves isn't someone you want to date. He's the guy your parents warn you to stay away from. Sure, he's a great guy to have your back and I don't know what I'd do without him, but I don't want you dating him. Ever. And because I want you to stay away from him, he'll try his hardest to get your attention and to date you.

You could be friends with Damon. He's so hung up on Shay, he would barely even notice you're female. I'm sure the two of them are going to get married. If anyone can make a relationship last through deployment, it's them.

Knox... I don't really know how to explain Knox. He's tough and looks like he's going to kill someone just with his glare. Really though, he's one of the nicest guys I've ever met and he's the person I want by my side while living through this hell.

I love being a SEAL, but the things we face on a daily basis are hard to say the least. The areas we were dropped into are even worse and I feel like you can never relax, even while sleeping, because we're constantly worried about someone attacking us.

Your letters help though, Hannah. Every time I get one, I can breathe a little easier knowing I'm fighting to protect you. I know I can talk to you and I know if something bad happens, someone in this world will actually care when I'm gone. You're a big light in this world of darkness. I thank God every day for your letters and your friendship.

Steele."

"Damn, that one got a little dark." I grimace and refuse to meet her gaze. I remember that time and how tough it was. I only had the guys and no family or friends at home. I almost didn't want to keep talking to Hannah, because I knew I'd become attached to her, but I couldn't stop either. It was nice having someone actually care about me.

"This letter…" she whispers. "This letter was the turning point. I knew I could never let you go. It broke my heart knowing I was the only person who cared about you. I vowed to myself I'd be there for you forever after I read it… I think I started falling in love with you in this letter."

"Really?"

"Yeah. You were raw and vulnerable with me. I loved that and I knew it wasn't easy for you. Something about being the good in someone's life made it more special too. I've never been that to anyone. My parents always acted like I was an annoyance to them. I was an obligation they didn't really want to deal with."

"I'm so sorry, Hannah Banana. You were never an obligation to me. I hope you know that. You were the most important person in my life. You were the thing that kept me going."

"Why did we fight meeting in person for so long?" She asks softly.

"I think I felt like you were too good to be true. There was no way our perfect relationship could continue in person. What we had was only special because it was on paper."

"Do you still believe that?"

"Absolutely not. What we have is special because it's between the two of us. It wasn't our circumstances, it was us. I'm sorry I pushed to keep our relationship in letters only. I never should've done that. I could've prevented you so much pain and misery if we had met sooner."

"Stop, Steely." She flashes me a cheeky grin when she uses my nickname. "Everything I went through was for a reason. Maybe I wouldn't have been ready for our relationship, or maybe you wouldn't be ready."

"Possibly." I shift in my seat and feel the object I've been carrying around for days.

"Dear Steele,

I look forward to our letters too, though I'm not afraid to admit how much. They're the highlight of my day. My week, really.

You don't need to worry about letting me in, Steele. I'm not going anywhere. I'm not sure I could give you up, even if I wanted to. You're like a drug and every letter I get is like another hit. You give me this high nothing else does.

I promise I'll stay far away from Rocco! I'm not sure I could handle someone like him anyway.

That's adorable how Damon's so in love with Shay. I've always wanted someone to love me like that. I can't even imagine what it's like.

Knox sounds... intense. I'd probably cry if we ever met in person. I don't do well with the scowler types. Maybe if I know he's nice then he won't scare me as much though.

Steele, I don't want anything bad to ever happen to you. I hate that you can't relax and you're always on edge. I wish I could do something to help. You can always talk and vent to me though. I feel a little honored to be the light of your life, I just wish I could do more. I'm always here for you, Steele. Always.

Love Hannah."

"That was the first time you signed *Love Hannah*." I peek up at her with a smile.

"Well, it was probably the first letter I wrote to you after I realized I loved you, even though I didn't really want to admit it to myself."

"I think we're finished," I say after another hour.

"Really?" Hannah glances over her shoulder at me.

"Yeah. It looks amazing. Take a look, then I'll wrap it up."

She jumps off the table and quickly rushes over to the mirror. She turns herself one way, then the other, taking in the entire design. From mid-thigh to the bottom of her ass is covered in a feminine tribal tattoo. It hides her old tattoo perfectly and she looks so sexy.

"I love it!" She throws herself into my arms and places a big kiss on my lips.

"Good. Let's get you wrapped up, then we can get out of here."

Hannah stands still as I place plastic over her skin to protect it. I quickly clean up my cubby as she gets dressed. When she's standing next to me, waiting for me to be done, I know this is the right time.

I tug her into my arms and tilt her chin back so I can claim her lips with my own. I swear I'm never going to get tired of her kisses or having her in my arms. I pull back and drop down onto my stool.

"What are you doing?" Hannah asks softly.

"Hannah Banana, I've loved you for years, long before we met. I dreamed of meeting you and always wondered if we would be as amazing off of paper as we were on paper. When you showed up in the shop, fuck baby, I had so many emotions coursing through me. I was ecstatic to see you, but I was so torn up over your injuries. I just wanted to hold you and protect you from all the bad in life. I don't think I let myself believe I was in love with you until that day. I always convinced myself that we just had a unique friendship, but I understood it was so much more than friendship the first time I laid eyes on you."

"Steele," she whispers as the first tear slips down her cheek.

"Hannah Banana, I'm sorry I can't drop to one knee for this, that would be a bit hard. But will you marry me and make me the happiest man in the world?"

"Yes!" She throws herself into my arms and almost knocks me off the stool. She straddles my lap and peppers my face with kisses, not caring one bit that all she's wearing is a thong and a tank top. "I love you so much. I can't wait to spend the rest of my life with you."

"Sweetheart, it's already started and it's going to be amazing."

Chapter 25
Hannah
One Year Later

Placing a hand on my lower back, I try to ease some of the ache. I'm glad I'm not working at the hospital today and instead I'm at Ink It Up.

"Are you ok, sweetheart?" Steele comes up behind me and begins rubbing my lower back. I let out a quiet groan as his thumbs dig in a little deeper.

"I'm just sore."

"Only a few more days. Are you going to make it?" He leans in and kisses the shell of my ear.

"I don't think I have much of a choice." I chuckle and lean back against Steele's chest. He wraps his arms around me and rests his hands on my massive belly.

"We get to meet him soon. Will that make it worth it?"

"Worth every second." I grin.

"Oh! Is he kicking? I want to feel!" Rocco races to my side and pushes Steele's hands out of his way so he can place his hands over my stomach.

"Go the fuck away. This is my wife and my baby." Steele shoves him out of the way. "Don't you have your own at home?"

"Yeah, but she told me not to touch her. Apparently getting her pregnant twice in one year is a no-no. She isn't happy with me." Rocco sticks out his bottom lip in a pout, making me chuckle.

"Maybe you need to stay away from Calan and stop following his lead." Steele rolls his eyes.

"You can't blame her. I've never given birth, but I don't think I'd want to do this twice so close together." I shrug.

"So, you'd push Steele away if he got you pregnant in three months?" Rocco quirks a brow.

"Nah, I'd never push my Man of Steele away." I smirk up at my wonderful husband.

"Will you stop calling him that! You make him sound like a superhero!" Rocco waves his hands in the air like he can erase my words from existence.

"Well, he kinda is a super hero. He's definitely my hero."

"Blah! Do you pay her to say this shit?" Rocco stares at Steele in disbelief. "No one in this world would ever call you a hero. I think they'd be more likely to call you the bad boy parents warn their daughters away from."

"Nah, that's you." Steele smirks as he kisses my cheek. "I'm done for the day. Are you ready to go home?"

"More than ready." I push myself off of the stool with a groan. "I swear getting up is harder and harder each day." I hold my lower back and take a second before I even try to move.

"Ummm..." Rocco frowns down at the floor as I freeze and slowly lower my gaze. "I don't think you should be heading home."

"Why?" Steele asks, sounding more than annoyed. Any time Rocco tries to touch my stomach, Steele's annoyed with him the rest of the day.

"Because I'm thinking you should go straight to the hospital since her water just broke."

Steele's eyes widen and he sucks in a sharp breath. He stares at me for a solid fifteen seconds before he rushes into his cubby like a hurricane.

"I always wondered how he'd respond when it was time." Rocco folds his arms over his chest and smirks.

"I had a feeling he'd kinda flip out," I say softly, not wanting Steele to overhear me.

"Oh, he's totally going to. I'm just wondering if he's going to hold it together or if he'll crumble?"

"He'll hold it together." Knox stands next to me and frowns down at the floor. "I'm not cleaning that up."

"Seriously, Knox?" I groan.

"Hey, I already had to clean up after Willow. I'm not doing it for you. You're not my wife." He shrugs.

"Holy shit, Knox. Can you be any more supportive?" Damon rolls his eyes. "I'll take care of it, sweetheart. Unlike Knox, I'm not afraid of cleaning up when a beautiful mama's water breaks." He winks at me.

"Ok. I've called the doctor. And the hospital. Dr. McLaren is going to meet us on the maternity floor. He said if your contractions aren't strong, you can go home and shower before you come in. How are they, Hannah Banana? Do you think we have time to get you cleaned up?" Steele reappears at my side with our things in his hands. His full attention is on me and nothing else.

"Uhh, yeah, I think. I don't really have contractions, just back pain." I rub at my lower back as another sharp pain rockets through me.

"Hate to break it to you, sweetheart, but you're having back labor." Knox smiles sadly. "Willow went through the same thing when she had Lilliana. She said it was rough."

"But we get to meet Flynn," Steele says softly as he places a hand on my lower back. "C'mon, darling, let's get home and then to the hospital."

"I'll meet you there!" Rocco smiles brightly.

"If you try to set foot in the delivery room, I'll fucking kill you." Steele points a finger in Rocco's face.

"Whoa there, Daddy Bear. I'm not going anywhere near the delivery room. I was thinking more of the waiting room until I'm politely invited to come back and see my nephew." Rocco holds up his hands and rolls his eyes like popping into the delivery room is something he'd never do... except he did. To Shay and Willow.

"I'm serious, Rocco. I let you get away with a lot of shit, but if you even try, I'm done with you," Steele growls.

"I won't let him out of my sight." Knox wraps an arm around Rocco's neck and pulls him into a playful chokehold.

"What is wrong with you!" Rocco slaps at Knox's arm, not trying very hard to get free.

"If you get out of here and to the hospital before I let him go, he won't be able to figure out which delivery room you're in."

Chapter 26
Steele

I've never felt like the world is a blur of activity around me, but right now it is. There are so many nurses coming in and out of the room, as well as Dr. McLaren. They each offer an easy smile and encouraging words, but my brain is spinning and the only thing I can focus on is my wife.

"Steele, I'm ok. Sit down and relax," Hannah says softly.

"What if you need something?"

"Then you can get up and get it for me." She giggles.

"Are you in pain?"

"No, that's what the epidural was for. Everything's going to be ok." She points to the chair next to her bed and holds out a hand to me. I reluctantly sit and take her hand in mine, but I'm not happy about this.

"You're not in any pain?" I peek up at her, not really believing she's comfortable.

"Not really. My back feels a hell of a lot better than it has in days. I'm still a little uncomfortable, but it's not nearly as bad." She squeezes my hand.

"Ok… How long is Flynn going to make us wait?" I grimace.

"As long as he wants to."

I step into the waiting room and all eyes snap to me. There are a few people here who don't belong to me, but the majority of them do.

"How's she feeling?" Willow is the first to stand with a sleeping Lilliana in her arms.

"She's great." I grin. I haven't been able to wipe my smile off my face since I set my gaze on my son.

"Damn, I don't think I've ever seen him so happy," Damon murmurs.

"Maybe they took the stick out of his ass while Hannah was in labor," Rocco chuckles like the asshole he is. "Ow, baby! What was that for?"

"Be nice for once in your life. Also, take the baby. I'm tired." Cammie hands over their little boy and places a hand on her lower back.

"Can we see Hannah and Flynn? I want to get back home before the baby wakes up. I know Charlie Robinson's more than able to handle the two kids, but I just hate being away from them." Shay laughs at herself and her dislike of being without her children.

"Of course. They were just moved to a room so they can have visitors now." I begin to lead them towards the elevator, but turn around to point in Rocco's face. "If you say one inappropriate thing while you're in that room, I'm going to punch you in the balls. Do you understand me?"

"Yes, fuck, Dad. Why can't you be cool?" Rocco rolls his eyes.

"Because you're obnoxious?" Willow asks with a cocky grin. I knew I liked her.

"What happened to the sweet woman we met years ago?" Rocco stares at her like she's a mystery. "I liked her much better."

"She told the world to go fuck itself and did whatever she wanted." Willow grins wider.

"Basically the Knox effect." Damon snorts with laughter.

"He does have a tendency of doing that to people." Cammie smirks as Knox flips her off. "Love you, big brother," she coos.

"Yeah, yeah. I love you too." He wraps an arm around her shoulders and presses a kiss to her temple.

"Is that what's wrong with Pit Bull?" Rocco muses.

"What's wrong with Pit Bull is that you keep knocking her up. She's tired and wants a break." Cammie glares at her husband.

"That's impossible. There's no way you're tired of my dick. It's amazing." Rocco frowns at her.

"Whatever you say, babe." Cammie rolls her eyes and Knox chuckles under his breath.

"Cammie! Take that back! You love me and every inch of me!"

"There aren't a whole lot of inches to love," I mutter, making everyone laugh.

"Excuse me!" Rocco spins around to glare at me.

"Oh, I'm sorry. Do you want me to repeat myself louder? I could make a banner so everyone on the maternity floor knows, if you'd like."

"I'll whip it out right now and show everyone just how many inches Cammie has to love?" He folds his arms over his chest and glares at me.

"No one wants to be scarred today." Shay grimaces.

"Or embarrassed," Cammie adds with a smirk.

"Oh, I'm going to spank you when we get home for that comment, baby. We both know there's nothing embarrassing about my cock."

"Ok. Ground rules before you're allowed to meet my baby." I glance at all of them, but let my eyes linger on Rocco. "No saying the word cock. No trying to check out my wife. No-"

"Blah, blah, blah. We get it. No having fun." Rocco rolls his eyes again.

"And be quiet." I sigh and scrub a hand down my face. I definitely need more sleep if I'm going to deal with Rocco for much longer. "Let me make sure she isn't feeding him."

"Dang, you really want to make sure we're not having *any* fun, huh?" Rocco mutters under his breath. I glare at him, but he's unfazed.

"Rocco, one day someone is going to punch you in the face and I'm not even going to blame them." Cammie shakes her head.

"Knox already did! And if I remember correctly, you broke his nose for it. So don't go acting like you don't care about me, because you do. You. Do."

I take a deep breath and push open the door to Hannah's room. She has Flynn in her arms and she's staring down at him with so much love in her gaze.

"Hey, sweetheart, are you ready for visitors?" I ask softly.

"Yeah, he just finished eating and fell asleep again." She brushes her fingers over his smooth cheek. "He's so adorable."

"You did a good job, Mama."

"Mmm, I like the sound of that." She grins up at me.

"I guess Hannah Banana is out and Mama is in?" I raise a brow.

"Hannah Banana isn't *out*, I just like Mama a little more right now. I'm sure when Flynn's walking around saying Mama nonstop, I won't be as fond of the name." She chuckles.

"Did you forget about us?" Rocco calls through the shut door. There's a loud smack followed by Rocco groaning about how Cammie's always mean to him.

"You better let them in before they kill Rocco."

"I mean... wouldn't that make our lives easier if he weren't in it?"

"Stop it!" Hannah giggles. "You love him and you know it. He's like a stupid little puppy. No matter how much you want to hate him when he's annoying, you can't because he stares at you with those big innocent eyes."

"We could always take him to the pound."

"Oh, you love him and you know it. Your life would be so boring without Rocco Reeves in it." She pushes me towards the door. "Let them in so they can visit before Flynn wakes up."

I let out a sigh and slowly walk towards the door. I do love my friends – family really – but I want some time alone with my new family. Can't they give me a year or two with them before they have to burst in to meet Flynn?

"C'mon, but be quiet. Flynn's sleeping." I eye Rocco, making sure he realizes I'm specifically talking to him.

He makes a zipping motion across his lips and pretends to secure a lock and then he tosses the invisible key in the air. I play along and lunge forward to grab the key out of the air and tuck it into my pocket, making his eyes light up with amusement. I don't know why I'm encouraging him.

"Oh my gosh! Look at how adorable he is!" Cammie coos. "I want another one." She sticks out her bottom lip.

Rocco motions wildly at her stomach, but everyone ignores him. They're going to take this silence and enjoy it for as long as they can.

"Um, Cams. Have you looked down? You're getting another one in a few weeks." I shake my head at her.

"I know, but they're so cute. I just want a whole slew of babies." She lets out a tiny sigh of happiness.

"Yeah, but remember, they're going to grow up," Damon points out.

"And they're half Rocco. Do we really need a whole slew of half Rocco's running around the world?" Knox eyes his sister like she's crazy. And maybe she is. There's no way a sane person would marry Rocco.

"Think of the future of humanity! You can't do that to mankind," I whisper yell.

Rocco flips us all off, but we continue to ignore him. It's only going to frustrate him and maybe he'll leave sooner.

Everyone visits and passes around Flynn. He's a happy little baby as he snores away, but when he starts fussing, I know it's time to cut this visit short.

"Alright, get out."

"Steele!" Hannah laughs. "Be nice."

"Nope. My boy wants his Mama and he wants to eat." I scoop Flynn out of Willow's hands and carry him over to my beautiful wife.

"Well, we better go before he literally shoves us out the door," Damon grumbles, but he's not upset. He's smirking the entire way to the door.

"Let us know if you need anything." Shay leans down to hug Hannah.

"Thank you. I just want to get home and settle into our new life."

"The first night is always the best." She waves before taking Damon's outstretched hand and following him out of the room. They're so happy together. I'm glad they found their way back to each other after everything they've been through.

Willow and Knox congratulate us and after handing out hugs, they follow Shay and Damon out.

I turn back to Hannah and grin as she leans down to press a gentle kiss to Flynn's cheek. While I'm distracted, a hand slips into my pocket and grazes my cock.

"What the fuck?" I slam my elbow into Rocco's stomach and he lets out a quiet groan.

He quickly pretends to unlock his lips with the imaginary key he just took out of my pocket and pants like he's out of breath.

"Damn, that was hard... kinda like Steele is."

"I'm not hard, you asshole." I roll my eyes.

"Seriously? Well, fuck. Then, Hannah, you're one lucky lady. Almost as lucky as Cammie." He snakes an arm around Cammie's waist and tugs her into his side.

As much as she likes to act annoyed, she's loving every second of it. She always has. Over the years, I've seen the way she's watched him. She's been in love with him for years, but she wasn't going to let anyone know that. Neither was Rocco.

If either one of them swallowed their pride and let their true feelings be known, they would've started dating years ago. I can only imagine how many kids they'd have by now if they hadn't waited so long to get married.

"Let's go, Roc. I'm sure they're ready to have some family time." Cammie places a hand on his chest and stares up at him with so much love. I don't think anyone could love him the way she does.

"But I'm family. Shouldn't I be involved in this family time?"

"No. C'mon, you remember what it was like when Lana was born." Cammie steps away from him and wraps me in a tight hug. "Congrats, Dad. Enjoy your new family." She places a quick kiss on my cheek before she moves to give Hannah a hug.

"Congratulations, Daddy. I'm proud of you, Steele." Rocco envelopes me in his arms.

"Proud of me for what?" I hug him back as my brows tug together.

"You found what you wanted and you held onto her with both hands. You found your happily ever after. I wasn't sure you would."

"Aww, were you worried about me?" I coo like the asshole I am.

"Yes." Rocco steps back and meets my gaze. "I wanted you to be as happy as the rest of us are. It was killing me to see everyone coupled up and starting their own families, except you. After everything you've been through, I wanted you to find a good woman to love you and you did that. Hannah's amazing and I'm so glad I signed you up for that program."

"What program?" I frown at him.

"The one where soldiers without family to write to them can find pen pals. I wasn't sure how it was going to turn out, but I'd say it was pretty fucking good." He folds his arms over his chest with a smirk.

"I knew it was you! You've denied it for ten years! Why?"

"I don't know." He shrugs a shoulder. "There was no reason you needed to know."

"Kinda like how you're the one that kept me alive?" I arch a brow.

"I told you, I don't like to talk about that day," he says softly. I know that day bothers him more than he lets people see. He shuts down every time it's brought up and tries to change the subject.

"He wanted you to feel like someone other than the guys loved you. He wanted you to have someone to write to so you weren't reminded of what pieces of shit your family was. And yes, he saved your life even though he tries to pretend it was a group effort, it wasn't." Cammie rolls his eyes.

"Why can't you keep your mouth shut?" Rocco frowns at his wife.

"Because I do what I want. I don't know why you constantly act like an ass when you're actually amazing, loving, and caring."

"I don't need recognition for the shit I do. I'm happy to just make peoples' lives a little better and silently knowing I did it. And you keep ruining that."

"Thank you, Rocco," Hannah says softly.

"For what?"

"Bringing the two of us together. Saving his life. Always being there for us. I could go on and on, but we both know you don't want to hear it." She smiles sweetly at him. "Did Steele tell you what Flynn's full name is?"

"No. Please tell me you didn't choose something stupid."

"His name is Flynn Rocco Camron," I say slowly, keeping my gaze locked on him the entire time.

"Seriously? You named him after me?" Tears begin welling in his eyes and he does nothing to stop them, even after they start trickling down his cheeks.

"Yes. Without you, he never would've been born. We wouldn't have found each other. Hell, I probably wouldn't even be alive."

"We owe all of our happiness to you," Hannah adds.

"And we'll never be able to thank you enough." I wrap him in another hug and chuckle when he grabs onto my shirt.

"Well, shit. Now you're making me cry too." Cammie swipes at her cheeks.

Author's Note

Thank you so much for reading Cover Up! I always hate ending a series, but I know this won't be the last you see of these guys. They'll pop up somewhere else for sure.

In fact, so many of the characters you met in Cover Up have their own books already!

Sammie and Cole – Blurred

Derek – Dr. Devine is Mine

Owen – Resisting the Bosshole

Ethan – Leading to Love

Calan – Rhythm of Love

Tyson – Managing Love

Quinn – Touring for Love

Stay Connected With Me

https://linktr.ee/Kristinmacqueenauthor

Also by Kristin MacQueen

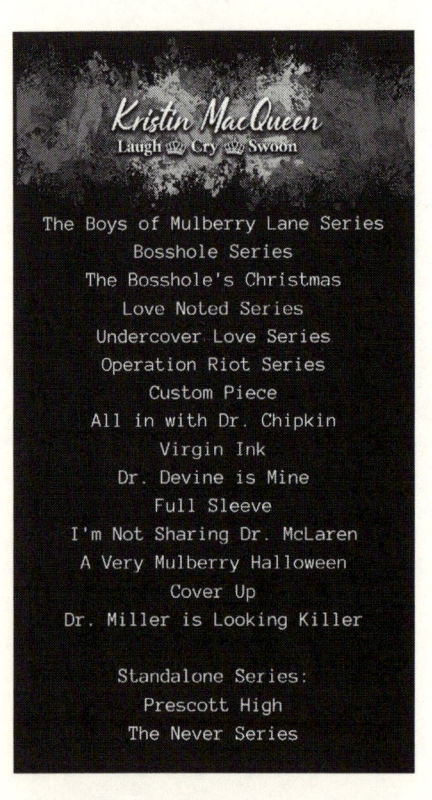

Kristin MacQueen
Laugh · Cry · Swoon

The Boys of Mulberry Lane Series
Bosshole Series
The Bosshole's Christmas
Love Noted Series
Undercover Love Series
Operation Riot Series
Custom Piece
All in with Dr. Chipkin
Virgin Ink
Dr. Devine is Mine
Full Sleeve
I'm Not Sharing Dr. McLaren
A Very Mulberry Halloween
Cover Up
Dr. Miller is Looking Killer

Standalone Series:
Prescott High
The Never Series

The Boys of Mulberry Lane

Believe
Bare
Broken
Bliss
Blessed
Blurred
Breathless
Bold

Never Series

Never Letting Go
Never Giving Up
Never Backing Down

The Bosshole Files

Assisting the Bosshole
Resisting the Bosshole
Distracting the Bosshole
The Bosshole's Christmas
A Very Mulberry Halloween

Love Noted

Love Noted Prequel - FREEBIE
To the Jerk in 4C
Dear Loser
To Whom It May Concern

Undercover Love

To Protect

To Serve

Ink It Up

Custom Piece
Virgin Ink
Full Sleeve
Cover Up

University Hospital

All-in with Dr. Chipkin
Dr. Devine is Mine
I'm Not Sharing Dr. McLaren
Dr. Miller is Looking Killer

Prescott High

If I Surrender
If I Cave
If I Stumble

Operation Riot

Leading to Love
Rhythm of Love
Managing Love
Touring for Love

Standalones

Under the Mistletoe
It's Always Been You
Unknown Caller – FREEBIE

Made in the USA
Columbia, SC
11 June 2024